I0645677

The Homecoming

LOWCOUNTRY SECRETS, BOOK 1

TYORA MOODY

TYMM PUBLISHING LLC

The Homecoming
Lowcountry Secrets, Book 1

Copyright © 2025 by Tyora Moody

All rights reserved. No part of this book may be reproduced or transmitted in any form or by any means without written permission of the author. Presumed Guilty is a work of fiction. Names, characters, places and incidents either are products of the author's imagination or are used fictitiously. Any resemblance to actual persons, living or dead, events, or locales is entirely coincidental.

Paperback ISBN: 978-1-961437-26-5

Ebook ISBN: 978-1-961437-99-9

Published by:
Tymm Publishing LLC
www.tymmpublishing.com

Editing: Felicia Murrell
Cover Design: TywebbinCreations.com

Part One

The Journey Home

Chapter 1

Panama City, Florida
Thursday, May 8 at 3:13 p.m. CST

"This is absolutely unacceptable."

Tracey Boyd pressed her fingers against her temple. The words sliced through her making the world spin as her emotions warred inside. All her hard work and this was how she was being treated. Despite her desire to tell this woman where she could go, Tracey willed her voice to remain steady and attempted to explain to her boss, "My son had a 102-degree fever. He can't go to school or daycare until he's better."

Regina Morrison's high-pitched voice cut through the phone, piercing Tracey's throbbing head. "We're pitching to Southeast Banking Association on Monday, and you've been out of the office for two days. Can't you find someone to help you?"

Tracey squeezed her free hand into a fist and pressed it firmly against her lips to prevent the retort that threatened to spill from her mouth. She desperately wanted to beat on the pillow that lay beside her on the couch, but she remained still, almost frozen in place.

It was one thing dealing with a woman who was clearly not qualified for her position, always leaning on Tracey for help, but this lack of empathy was about to push her over the edge. She'd always been aware of the stark differences in her life compared to her boss's. Being raised and married into wealth, Regina's high-strung personality demanded that everything go her way. The woman had a nanny to take care of her three children so she could be a pretend superwoman.

Though Tracey couldn't see her on the phone, she imagined the tall, slender woman with her perfectly coiffed, golden blonde hair pacing her office. During their face-to-face confrontations in Regina's oceanfront office, Tracey often stared out the floor-to-ceiling windows at the endless horizon, longing to escape. Right now, she wanted to escape this conversation and get off the phone.

Proving how tone-deaf she really was, Regina droned on. "Everyone has personal problems. My Joey had a bug a few weeks ago too, but I had to go to Atlanta. It couldn't be avoided. Do you think the hurricane cared about our personal problems? Do you think our competitors care? The Morrison needs this convention to stay afloat."

The Morrison, Regina's family's hotel, had been limping along since Hurricane Dora slammed into Panama City Beach last August. The luxury boutique hotel wasn't a stranger to storms, but this last one wreaked considerable damage, leaving the oceanfront wing still hidden behind construction barriers and temporary supports. With Memorial Day weekend less than three weeks away, this executive retreat could mean the difference between sinking or swimming.

The hurricane had been scary, but Tracey wasn't a stranger to these types of storms. Growing up in Beaufort, South Carolina, she had vivid memories of extensive damage caused by strong winds and flooding. But Hurricane Regina, the year-round storm system causing havoc in her life, had started to take a toll. When her old boss, Lauren Morrison, announced her retirement, appointing her niece as her replacement, Tracey instinctively knew Regina would be trouble. Her only qualifications were the fact that she grew up around the hotel *her* family owned.

Tracey unclenched her fist and shook her hand to loosen the tension. She knew what was at stake here. But life had been 'lifing' with one thing after the other. Despite her own frustrations, Tracey tried to allay her boss's concern. Again. That task had become a permanent part of her job description. "Regina, I understand that, and I have —"

"You realize the east wing renovations depend on securing these bookings," Regina steamrolled into her next gripe. "If we lose Southeast Banking, we'll lose credibility with being able to sell our upscale, premier destination."

Tracey rolled her eyes. *Lord, deliver me from overdramatic women. This heffa was using her words.* Words she'd crafted as the marketing coordinator for the website and marketing brochures. Tracey tried again to ease her boss's anxiety. "I've been working remotely, Regina. The presentation is nearly—"

Regina snapped. "Send it to me. I need to see what you've been working on. And, Tracey, tomorrow is Friday. I expect you in the office. We have to be ready on Monday. Jasper Cunningham is flying in from Miami on Sunday. My father and I will wine and dine the bank's vice president. But Monday morning, you need to do what we pay you to do."

"I will—" The call ended abruptly leaving Tracey staring at her phone.

I know she didn't just hang up on me!

Tracey threw her phone onto the couch and placed her trembling hands on the sides of her face. Before she could stop herself, a long moan slipped from her throat. Her neck and shoulder muscles ached as if she'd just finished a rigorous workout. Regina knew she'd been working non-stop outside of the office. With her toxic boss breathing down her neck, Tracey had no choice but to answer work emails and calls.

This job had not always been like this. When she first accepted the position five years ago, it had been a godsend. Back then, her boss had been a ray of sunshine. But she'd retired and now Tracey was always working after hours, burning the midnight oil. She was stressed out of her mind, trying to entice visitors to come to the Morrison to relax and unwind on their vacations and retreats.

Lord, when am I going to get a break?

The presentation wasn't as perfect as she liked it to be, but Tracey saved the PowerPoint. It would have to do. She attached the slides to an email to Regina and thumped the enter key on her laptop a bit too hard. She really didn't need this kind of pressure. In the last few months, she'd perused open positions online, something she wouldn't have fathomed doing until a year ago.

After leaving a painful past, Tracey had built a life in this town for her and her son. The ordeal of picking up and moving made her click away from other possibilities. But how long could she continue to endure? Tracey loved working at the Morrison, but Regina had become increasingly worse. No one liked the woman and only tolerated her because she was a Morrison.

Tracey stood from the couch and stretched. She had a few hours before the workday officially ended but wanted to check on her son. Jayden's fever had lingered this morning, leaving her no choice but to keep him home one more day. He'd eaten the chicken soup and soup crackers for lunch, and she was relieved to see his appetite return. She hoped he would fully recover enough to return to school tomorrow.

She'd left Jayden's bedroom door slightly ajar so she could hear him if he awoke. Peeking through the bedroom door, she could see Jayden sleeping soundly. His stuffed Snoopy was wrapped in one arm and his toy Spiderman lay by his side. That first night, the fever had brought the young boy vivid nightmares.

Tracey had to face her own waking nightmare, a boss she despised. Still too riled up to return to her laptop, she decided on a cup of mint tea. While she waited for the water in the electric kettle to boil, she washed the dirty dishes in the sink instead of sticking them in the dishwasher. The almost too warm soapy water felt good on her skin. By the time she finished with the dishes, the kettle clicked off and the hot water settled.

While the tea bag steeped, she glanced over at the pile of mail on the kitchen table. For the past few days, she'd brought it in but hadn't bothered to look through it. Tracey picked up her mug and shuffled over to sort through the pile. Most of it could be shredded or thrown in the trash. All her bills were paid online, so there were no paper invoices or statements.

One piece of mail, a plain white envelope, stood out. Maybe because it didn't scream, "You've been pre-selected to go deeper into debt with a shiny new credit card." Or even more insulting, entice her with consolidating all her debt with a high interest loan offer.

Tracey frowned at the return address. Then, the anger she'd felt a few moments ago stirred. This time the rekindled fury brought memories of pain and shame she'd left behind. She thought she'd buried those emotions and moved on. Her hand trembled as she touched the envelope.

Darrell Boyd #149587

Lieber Correctional Institution

Why would he reach out now?

The backlash of his conviction had shattered her life. Folks she'd never dreamed would turn on her, had shown their true colors.

Could she blame them?

She was the daughter of a murderer.

They say forgiveness is for yourself, not the other person. But Tracey could not accept what her father had done. He'd crushed *her*, and her life had never been the same. There was nothing he could ever say, no amount of explaining. He deserved to be locked inside *that* cell for the rest of his life.

Tracey had packed up what was left of her life, a life that included a young son she needed to protect. After losing

Jayden's father, Jordan, in a car accident, and then having her own father charged with murder just a few months later, Tracey had no choice but to start fresh somewhere else. Jayden had been too young to understand what happened to his father or grandfather. So for the past five years, Tracey had made this place home.

For her father to reach out after all this time, she was pretty sure her Aunt Edna had something to do with that. Her aunt had promised to never share Tracey's address. Why did she break that promise? Tracey could avoid her father, but she couldn't ignore her father's older sister. Aunt Edna had become the mother figure in her life after Tracey's mama died.

Mama had been the glue of the family. Tracey often wondered if her mama was still alive would her father have resorted to violence.

She drank her now tepid tea as past memories invaded her thoughts. There was a time when she loved her father and would never have thought him capable of hurting a fly. Definitely not another human being. She'd long since stopped trying to understand and just settled for not caring, pushing the past behind her.

She rinsed out the mug and placed it in the sink. On the way out of the kitchen, she reached for the letter and took it to her bedroom. Tracey had no intention of opening the letter, although something in the back of her mind urged her not to ignore it. Instead, she laid it on her dresser and headed back to the living room.

She had work to do. The past would have to wait.

Chapter 2

The fortress of cement and steel, with its barbed-wire fences, greeted Emmett Craig as he pulled into the parking lot at Lieber Correctional Institution. It wasn't his first time here, but it never got easier walking into the lion's den. The facility had a reputation of holding some of the most violent criminals in South Carolina. At one time, it was the place where death row inmates were held. The inmate he was going to visit was serving a life sentence in the maximum security prison.

If Emmett's mentor hadn't left this case for him, he wouldn't be here. But he owed a lot to the man who'd inspired him to become a lawyer. Andrew McMillan might have been short in stature, but he was sharp, and smart on his feet, sealing his reputation with dozens of prosecutors. Mr. Mac taught Emmett to never quit, which was exactly what he wanted to do after what happened with his last case.

Being a defense attorney was not the most popular profession, but everyone deserved representation in the courtroom and were innocent until proven guilty in a court of law. Emmett just hadn't realized the client he'd valiantly fought for six months ago *should be* behind bars here at Lieber. What was done could not be corrected, at least not without Emmett throwing away his career. All he could do was shoulder the guilt and pray for redemption.

Is that what Mr. Mac had in mind? Emmett had no idea his mentor would be gone from this earth, passing on his remaining caseload to him. Neither of Mr. Mac's children were lawyers, so no one objected to what Emmett had inherited. Being a defense attorney was not the most popular profession.

He sighed and adjusted his tie. "I'm doing this for you, Mr. Mac."

As soon as Emmett cut the engine, the blazing sun quickly heated the car. Despite it being May, the day was a scorcher. He grabbed his briefcase from the passenger seat before climbing out of his navy blue BMW. The air wrapped around him slightly fogging his glasses. After wiping them on his shirt, he strode toward the prison entrance.

A guard at the entrance gave him a once-over. "State your business."

Emmett forced a tight smile. "Emmett Craig. I'm here to see Darrell Boyd."

The guard grunted, his eyes boring holes into him. Emmett started to wonder if the guard had recognized his name. The court case late last year brought him a lot of media attention and not for good reasons. He guessed the guard, who appeared to be in his fifties, wasn't far away from his pension. Emmett practically held his breath, but the guard dropped his eyes, seeming to lose interest.

"Sign in. Empty your pockets."

Relieved, Emmett signed the visitor log, surrendered his briefcase, and walked through the metal detector. The tension returned full force as he gritted his teeth through the pat-down. With his briefcase back in his possession, Emmett followed a younger corrections officer down a sterile hallway. The meeting room was small and bare. A metal table was bolted to the floor with two chairs facing each other. Without any windows, the fluorescent lights cast the room in a yellowish tone.

"Boyd will be out in a minute," the officer said, closing the door behind him.

Emmett set his briefcase on the table and sat down, trying to quiet his thoughts. He'd reviewed Darrell Boyd's file multiple times. Convicted of murdering his business partner seven years ago, the evidence had been damning enough for a jury to put him away. Yet, Darrell had always maintained his innocence.

They all did, didn't they? Even when it wasn't true.

The door opened, and Darrell Boyd shuffled in, his hands and ankles shackled. Looking thinner and worse than he did at their first meeting a week ago, if that was possible, the man's prison jumpsuit hung loose on his frame. His dark skin had taken on an ashy gray pallor indicative of his advanced illness. At fifty-seven, his appearance had changed drastically from previous photographs Emmett had seen of the man Darrell had been prior to his conviction.

"Mr. Craig." Darrell's voice rasped as he lowered himself carefully into the chair. "You came back. Even after I insulted you."

Emmett smiled, recollecting Darrell's initial shock at seeing him. He was used to it by now. It was the story of his life, a little skinny white boy who always seemed to attract bullies. And how he'd met Mr. Mac. His son, Kenny, had become Emmett's protector on the playground. One day Kenny invited Emmett to his house where he'd met the man who'd become a father figure and mentor.

Out of all the cases Mr. Mac had left him, Darrell Boyd's case stood out. The man had stage four colon cancer. And despite his sentence, a maximum security prison without adequate medical care was not the place for a terminally ill man.

"I said I would come back." Emmett leaned forward. "The oncologist I spoke with is willing to review your case, but we need to move quickly to get you transferred to Beaufort Memorial."

Darrell's sunken eyes focused intently on Emmett's face. "I'm not worried about treatment. Did you talk to my Tracey?"

Emmett hesitated. "Mr. Boyd—"

"Call me Darrell, please."

"Darrell, I haven't made contact yet." From what Emmett could ascertain, Darrell's daughter left the state with her son and had not been back to visit her father. Emmett didn't have the best relationship with his own now deceased father, so he wasn't one to judge.

Darrell's cuffed hands clenched. "I need to see her before—" He stopped, swallowing hard. "The doctors say four months, maybe six. I can't die with her thinking I killed James. I can't."

Emmett studied the man across from him. After his last case, Emmett had promised himself he wouldn't be fooled again by a smooth-talking client. But there was something in Darrell's eyes that spoke of desperation beyond just wanting freedom. The man was more concerned about connecting with his daughter and proving his innocence before he died.

"Tell me again what happened that night," Emmett opened his briefcase and took out a legal pad.

Darrell took a shuddering breath. "James and I were arguing about the business. The construction company was losing money—not because of anything we did wrong. Our biggest client went bankrupt and left us holding the bag for materials and labor. James wanted to declare bankruptcy. I wanted to try to save our company."

Emmett nodded, making notes as Darrell continued.

"We were at the office late. I left around nine. James was still there, going over the books. The next morning, they found him with his head bashed in, the safe open and empty." Darrell's voice cracked. "They found the money and the paperweight in my truck. But I swear to you, Mr. Craig, I didn't do it. I've done some stupid things in my life. But if I killed the man, I surely wouldn't have left a trace that I did it."

Emmett did feel like Darrell had been framed. The finding of the evidence was almost too obvious.

"The prosecution's case hinged on opportunity, motive, and the physical evidence," Emmett said. "If we're going to file an appeal, we need something new—evidence that wasn't available at the trial. Knowing Mr. Mac like I did, I know he turned over every possible leaf."

"I don't doubt Mac did what he could, but there was a lot riding against him and this case. Most of Beaufort had already decided that I was guilty. People were determined to make me pay for this crime. Mac had a hard time with the jury selection and they wouldn't move the trial out of town." Darrell grimaced, a spasm of pain crossed his features.

Concerned, Emmett reached out as if he could help the man. He had to get Darrell out of this place. He didn't need to suffer like this. "Are you getting any medication?"

A wry grin appeared on Darrell's face, and he waved as if the pain was nothing to him. "When they remember. The pain comes and goes. Mostly comes the past few days."

Emmett stood. "I'll file a motion for medical transfer today. And I'll reach out to your daughter. She should know what's going on with you."

The guard knocked on the door, signaling their time was up.

Emmett walked out of the prison, the not guilty verdict he had secured last fall weighed heavily on his conscience during his dreams and his waking hours. Emmett knew that man truly deserved to go to prison. The backlash on social media and the victim's angry family only added to his despair.

Now, he was about to fight to free another murderer.

But Darrell Boyd was dying. If the man was guilty, he wouldn't be around long enough to inflict pain on anyone.

Beaufort, South Carolina
Thursday, May 8 at 10:38 p.m. EST

The cardboard container of chicken lo mein had gone cold hours ago. After Emmett spread Darrell Boyd's case files across his dining room table, he'd forgotten to finish eating. Tired from a long day, he sat back and rubbed his eyes. Darrell's gaunt face continued to haunt him long after he left the prison.

Emmett stood to stretch his legs. To get his mind off the case, he sauntered over to check his DIY handiwork. He'd inherited the family home after his father died two years ago. At first he wasn't sure he wanted it. But after being back in Beaufort, he figured having a mortgage free home wasn't a bad bargain. He'd put his hard earned money into renovating the old house. Even though it was the house where he grew up, adding fresh coats of paint provided an opportunity for him to put his stamp on the place. It was also an attempt to free himself of old memories.

Emmett's dad, Richard Craig had been a hard man to live with. It was no wonder Emmett stayed away as much as he could. His dad died with the same curmudgeon attitudes he'd hung onto most of his life. He'd often wondered if it had to do with losing his mother. But then he remembered how his dad treated his mother before she died.

His mind slipped back to Darrell's desperation to reach out to his daughter. At least the man wanted to fix what went wrong in their relationship, where Emmett's dad didn't seem to care. Tracey Boyd wasn't the only one with daddy issues.

Tracey's name tugged at his conscience. He felt like he knew her. Emmett went over to the stacks of boxes in the corner of the living room. He'd replaced the furniture in the living room but still had a long way to go before things became comfortable in *his* home.

He found the box he was looking for at the very bottom of the stack. Kneeling down, Emmett pulled open the flap and rummaged through before extracting his high school yearbook from his senior year. The only yearbook he'd ever elected to purchase. The binding cracked as he opened it. He flipped through the pages with an image in mind. Finally, he reached the sophomore class.

It was her!

All these years later and he would reconnect with *this* *Tracey*. A long forgotten memory of a crush he'd once had stirred. Her caramel skin, sparkly brown eyes, and shy smile had intrigued him back then. It didn't hurt that she was pretty smart too. She'd been friends with Charlene McMillan, always hanging around the Mac family home when he was there.

"Would she remember me?" he murmured, tracing a finger over the photograph. He wondered what she looked like now being the mother of a young son. How had life treated her with her father convicted of a murder he claimed he didn't commit? She apparently didn't know her father was dying of cancer in prison. If she did by chance remember Emmett, what would she think of him taking on her father as a client?

A sharp crack outside jerked him from his thoughts. It wasn't the sound of the old house settling but something else. His security app chimed with an alert on his phone. Emmett set the yearbook aside, pulled the phone out of his pocket and tapped the notification.

After moving back into the house, his friend Kenny helped him find a good security company in the area. His father never saw the need for a security system, despite the neighborhood always having some bad characters. Emmett's reason for the security system went beyond deterring neighborhood burglaries.

He stared intently at the screen. Was he seeing what he thought he saw? Was that something or someone moving just at the edge of the camera's range? He zoomed in, but the image pixelated.

The dogs next door began barking.

Emmett's throat tightened.

A thought flashed in his mind.

Preston Langley's face in the courtroom when the jury had declared him not guilty. The smugness in Langley's eyes had confirmed what Emmett already knew in his gut. The man had killed and gotten away with it because of a technicality Emmett exploited.

When they'd shaken hands after the verdict, Langley leaned over and whispered. "Thanks for the get-out-of-jail-free card, Counselor."

Emmett had known fear growing up with a mean drunk for a dad. But he always had an uneasy feeling about representing Langley. Enough people had warned him, including Mr. Mac. If Emmett's mother or grandmother had still been alive, he was sure they would have warned him too.

Usually when Emmett made rash decisions, it cost him. Emmett felt desperate and made himself believe he needed the case. Coming back to town after working in an Atlanta law firm all those years, he didn't want to throw away his hard-earned career.

But Langley had been and still was a crooked businessman. And now Emmett was bound by attorney-client confidentiality for the rest of his life.

Most people were not fooled by the jury verdict. The backlash from the Langley verdict had been swift and merciless. It wasn't the angry phone calls, emails and social media posts. Emmett easily ignored all of that. It was Arnold Sullivan; the victim's brother had made the acquittal personal.

Sullivan cornered Emmett in the courthouse parking lot after the jury's decision. The former Marine jabbed his thick finger in Emmett's face. "You helped a murderer walk. How do you plan to sleep at night?"

The truth was, Emmett hadn't slept well for almost six months. He'd always been a night owl, but some nights he struggled with insomnia.

For all the trouble with Sullivan, Emmett hadn't heard a peep from Langley after the invoices were settled. And he'd been paid incredibly well. Had the money been worth it? Emmett wasn't so sure.

For weeks after the trial, Sullivan had shown up at local spots where Emmett ate lunch and lingered outside Emmett's small downtown office. Once, he'd even approached Emmett outside the grocery store, his voice steady, eyes burning with grief and rage. "My brother's killer walks free because of you."

Emmett had filed a police report, but there was little they could do since Sullivan hadn't touched him. It also didn't help that the Sullivans had a reputation. The victim, Bobby Sullivan, had been Beaufort's golden boy, a star quarterback who led the Eagles to their only state championship before heading to Clemson on a football scholarship.

When an injury ended his NFL dreams, he'd returned home, started a real estate business and poured himself into the community. Kids wore his old jersey number. He coached youth football on weekends and sponsored half the little league teams in the county. His annual golf tournament, a popular charity event, raised thousands for the children's hospital.

And Emmett had helped his killer walk free. He'd heard the funeral had drawn nearly the entire town. On social media, a reel went viral of Bobby's widow and their three young children standing stoically as the casket was lowered into the ground.

The Langley case was supposed to be Emmett's big splash in Beaufort, a chance to establish himself in his hometown after his father's death. Instead, it had made him a controversial figure, dividing the community between those who admired his legal prowess and those who questioned his ethics.

A few nights ago, he thought he'd glimpsed Arnold Sullivan watching his house from a parked pickup truck down the street. When Emmett approached, the truck drove away leaving him unsure. But the distinct build of the dark figure inside looked familiar to him. Like his deceased brother, Sullivan had the broad shoulders of a former football player.

Emmett felt like Langley should get the brunt of Sullivan's anger. His former client lived behind iron gates in a luxurious home. He, on the other hand, lived in his childhood home that he'd been slowly renovating to be his sanctuary.

Emmett sprinted upstairs to his bedroom. His room was dark except for the moonlight spilling through the window. He skirted around the bed to the nightstand and pulled open the drawer. He hated that he felt the need to do this, but he withdrew his handgun anyway. He'd never fired the Glock outside a shooting range.

Weird. All the time he'd lived in Atlanta, Emmett never felt the need to have a gun, and then he moved back home.

But the last case had changed his life in more ways than he cared to admit. He trotted back down the stairs and checked the security camera on his phone. Everything appeared quiet outside.

He could be overreacting.

But he gripped the cold steel in his hand.

Better to be prepared.

Chapter 3

Panama City, Florida
Friday, May 9 at 7:45 a.m. CST

Tracey knew she needed to calm down while driving, but she seethed every time her cell phone pinged. She knew who it was, but she had no intentions of responding to Regina.

I expect you to be in the office this morning. No excuses.

All the years she'd given the Morrison, Tracey didn't deserve to be berated. She rarely took a day off, worked long hours each day, and never took a vacation. She had the right to be at home with her son when he didn't feel well. Thank God Jayden woke up before the alarm clock this morning. He was in her room ready to go to school.

"Jayden, are you sure you feel okay?" Tracey asked for the third time as she pulled into the school drop-off lane. Even though he seemed back to himself, she couldn't help worrying.

"I'm fine, Mama," Jayden whined and then proceeded to cough. Tracey's brow furrowed with concern.

"That cough doesn't sound 'fine' to me." She reached across to feel his forehead, but Jayden ducked away.

"Mama! I'm not hot anymore. You said I could go to school if my fever was gone." He clutched his Spider-Man backpack on his lap, clearly eager to escape the car and her fussing.

Tracey hesitated, checking the time on the dashboard. If she kept Jayden home another day, Regina would probably threaten to fire her on the spot. Tracey had no doubt Regina hated how dependent she was on her to make all this come together. The feelings were mutual.

"Okay, but promise you'll tell your teacher if you start feeling bad."

"I promise." Jayden's face brightened as she pulled up to the curb. He was out of the car almost before she stopped completely.

"Wait! Your lunch!" She held out the Spider-Man lunchbox he'd almost forgotten.

Jayden ran back and grabbed it. "Bye, Mama!"

Tracey watched him dash toward his friends, a pang of guilt hit her as he disappeared through the school doors. She pulled away from the school, her mind on autopilot as she reentered morning traffic. Was she sending Jayden back too soon just to appease Regina?

Or was she being overprotective because of everything else weighing on her mind, like the unopened letter from her father still sitting on her dresser? She'd glanced at the envelope several times this morning, each time wondering what her father had to say after all these years. It had to be something serious; she'd made her Aunt Edna promise to never share her new location with her father.

Tracey pulled into the employee parking lot in the back of the hotel and cut the engine. Sunlight drifted through the windshield penetrating her body. She sat, letting the warmth settle her raging nerves.

Lord, please help me today.

Tracey climbed out of the car and headed toward the hotel. After swiping her badge, she entered the side entrance. From the office suite, she glimpsed the hotel lobby. Morning light streamed through the tall windows, accentuating the nautical-inspired decor that made the Morrison a favorite among upscale tourists. Despite her frustrations with Regina, Tracey couldn't help but feel a sense of pride in the work she'd done to highlight the old hotel's charm.

Before Tracey could set her bag down in her small office, Regina was at her door. "Finally. The presentation looks decent, but we need to add more about the new amenities in the east wing."

Tracey didn't even try to wipe the frown off her face. "The east wing that isn't finished yet?"

"It will be by the time they host their event," Regina snapped. "Besides, the mockups from the designer look magnificent. I need you to incorporate them this morning. We will plan to practice the presentation in front of my father."

Not trusting herself to speak, Tracey nodded. She watched Regina's retreating form, noticing the woman's perfectly pressed pantsuit and not a blonde hair out of place. How the woman managed to look so put together while being so unraveled on the inside was beyond Tracey.

She's the epitome of a grown up mean girl!

Settled at her desk, Tracey was pulling up the slides when a soft knock came at her door. Mia Lopez, the department's administrative assistant, peeked her head in with a warm smile.

She slipped into Tracey's office with a paper coffee cup in hand and closed the door behind her. Approaching Tracey's desk with her arm extended, she said. "I saw Hurricane Regina blow through here. Figured you might need reinforcements."

Tracey accepted the cup gratefully, inhaling its rich aroma. "Mia, you're a lifesaver."

"Breakfast blend with two creams and two sugars." Mia perched on the edge of the chair across from Tracey's desk. "How's Jayden doing?"

The genuine concern in Mia's voice made her shoulders relax slightly. "He was bouncing off the walls this morning. He couldn't wait to get back to school."

"Kids are resilient that way." Mia had two children of her own, both teenagers now. She often shared stories of their exploits, providing Tracey with a glimpse of what she had to look forward to in the coming years.

Tracey nodded. "I wanted to keep him home another day. Let him have the weekend to fully recover."

"But then the Queen Bee would have had a complete meltdown," Mia rolled her eyes. "Honestly, the woman has three kids. She should understand, but she's the main one fussing when any of us have to be out of the office for family."

"She has a nanny," Tracey reminded her, taking a long sip of the coffee. "And a housekeeper. And probably someone to cut her food for her."

They shared a quiet laugh easing more of Tracey's tension. Having folks like Mia in the office made her days bearable.

"How's the Southeast Banking presentation coming along?" Mia's expression became more serious. "Henry was talking it up at yesterday's staff meeting. Sounds like it's a big deal."

"It is. If we land this contract, it'll cover a significant chunk of the east wing renovations." Tracey turned her computer screen to show Mia the slides she'd been working on. "But Regina wants me to include features that aren't even built yet."

"Ah, yes, the 'sell it before it exists' strategy." Mia shook her head. "Remember when they had me booking rooms in the west pavilion while the contractors were still installing the plumbing?"

Tracey rolled her eyes. "At least the toilets worked by check-in."

"Barely!" Mia giggled. "I should get back before Regina notices I'm fraternizing with the marketing coordinator." She paused at the door. "Hang in there, Tracey. If you need to duck out early for Jayden, text me. I'll run interference."

"Thanks, Mia. For the coffee and the pep talk."

After Mia left, Tracey turned back to her computer and opened the designer's mockups Regina had emailed. The designs were fabulous, but she still felt uncomfortable including them in the presentation. It seemed premature. Things happened with contractors all the time, and delays were bound to happen.

As she worked, her mind kept drifting to the envelope on her dresser at home. What could her father possibly have to say after all these years? And why now?

Friday, May 9 at 11:35 a.m. CST

As the morning wore on, Regina interrupted twice, popping in with additional suggestions that were really silly demands. By lunchtime, Tracey had a throbbing headache. Either she had caught what her son suffered from the past few days or she was just sick and tired of her boss.

Probably the latter.

There wasn't much time for lunch. But bless Mia, she'd ordered turkey wraps with chips and had them delivered. Tracey closed her door and locked it. She was sad she needed to do that, but Regina had crossed her boundaries one too many times the past few days, not including this morning since she walked in the door.

Tracey ate her wrap and checked her phone. Thankfully, there were no messages from Jayden's school. At least something was going right today. Then her phone buzzed in her hand. Puzzling over the unfamiliar number with a South Carolina area code, her stomach lurched. Aunt Edna and her best friend Charlene McMillan were the only two people from back home who ever called—and this wasn't either of their numbers.

Tracey debated letting it go to voicemail, guessing it could be one of those tricky robo-calls. But what if something happened to Aunt Edna and someone was trying to reach her? She answered the call as if tearing a band-aid off a wound. "Hello?"

"Is this Tracey Boyd?" a deep male voice asked.

She frowned. "Yes, who is this?"

"Ms. Boyd, my name is Emmett Craig. I'm your father's lawyer. I'm not sure if you know Mr. Mac...McMillan passed away earlier this year."

"Yes, I know. My aunt told me." Tracey's grip on her phone tightened. "What I don't understand is why you're calling about my father's case. He's serving life without parole."

"I inherited Mr. Mac's cases," the man explained. "He was working on your father's case before he passed."

The room seemed to tilt slightly as Tracey steadied herself against her desk. This was unexpected. Why was Mr. Mac, and now this new lawyer working on her father's case? Was it being reopened after all these years?

Her father's new lawyer cleared his throat. "I really didn't want to address this over the phone, but your father has been trying to reach you for some time. There are some things we need to discuss, things that he wants to discuss with you. It's rather urgent at this point."

Tracey's heart raced thinking of the unread letter she'd left on her dresser at home. "What's going on?"

The lawyer paused. "Your father has fallen ill. He wants to set things straight before..."

Tracey's eyes welled with tears. The man who had taught her to ride a bike, who had held her when her mother died, who had been her rock until he shattered their world. Was this man trying to say her father was dying?

"Ms. Boyd, could you come to South Carolina?"

Her tongue felt thick in her mouth. "Wh-When?"

"As soon as possible. Your father really wants to see you. I'm working on getting him transferred so he can receive better medical treatment."

Better medical treatment? For what?

Tracey didn't know how to respond, so she said nothing. Going back would mean facing not just her father but also memories of Jordan. Jayden's father, her high school sweetheart, left the world too soon in a car accident. And then there was Jordan's family. She'd never considered they would have turned on her the way they did.

The silence stretched between them until the lawyer spoke again. "I'm sorry to have to call you with this news."

She stammered. "Hmm, well... Thank you for calling. I'm at work, so I need to go."

After the call ended, Tracey stared out the window at the sparkling Gulf waters. Tears streamed down her cheeks as reality hit her. Was her father really dying? She had grieved him once already, on the day of his sentencing. Now she would grieve for him again. This time for good.

Her computer pinged with a Microsoft Teams message from Regina asking about the revised presentation. Tracey ignored it, trying to process the phone call. She'd worked so hard to make a home outside of her once beloved hometown. How would she explain to her toxic boss that she needed time off? She would have to pull Jayden out of school. With it being so close to the end of the school year, should she just wait? The lawyer made it sound like there was no time.

Was she ready to face her father after all these years?

Chapter 4

Beaufort, South Carolina
Friday, May 9 at 5:20 p.m. EST

Emmett pulled his BMW into the driveway of the Sweet-grass Bed-and-Breakfast. A wooden sign swung gently in front of the two-story Victorian home. Though the wraparound porch adorned with blue rocking chairs and luscious hanging ferns welcomed all visitors, he'd called ahead.

From his first meeting with Edna Mae Boyd three weeks ago, he didn't just want to drop in unannounced, especially when it came to discussing her baby brother's case. Edna had been the one to hire Mr. Mac, and she'd never quit fighting for her brother. She seemed to be the only family fighting for Darrell's innocence.

The phone call this morning with the younger Boyd woman weighed on Emmett's mind. He felt guilty about breaking the news of her father's illness. Would she make the trek home? That was one item on his list to talk about with her aunt.

As soon as Emmett started to climb the porch steps, the screen door opened. Edna stood in the doorway wearing a blue apron over a floral print dress. Her salt and pepper afro framed her face like a halo. She stood a foot shorter than his 6'1, but her fierce brown eyes assessed him. Emmett stopped at the top of the steps, resisting the urge to shrink under the woman's gaze. He'd learned she was a former teacher, and that authoritative stance hadn't left the woman, even though she now ran a bed-and-breakfast.

"Mr. Craig. Good to see you again." Despite her stern look, her Southern accent was warm and inviting.

"Thank you for seeing me, Mrs. Boyd."

"Miss Boyd," she corrected. She gave him a small smile as if he'd passed some test. "Come on in. I'm in the middle of baking, so we'll talk in the kitchen."

Whatever Edna was baking, the heavenly smell caressed his nose as he stepped inside. The entryway opened up to a sitting room furnished with a couch and several high-back chairs. Books were arranged on various bookshelves. A large bamboo ceiling fan spun overhead, creating a pleasant breeze. In the corner was a tall desk with a computer monitor. Emmett determined the area must serve as the guests' check-in.

"Do you have guests coming?" He asked.

"Yes, an older couple will be arriving this evening. They've stayed here before." Edna led him toward the back of the house and into a large kitchen. "Sweet tea? I just brewed a fresh pitcher."

"Tea would be fine, thank you."

She gestured to the island where several barstools lined the front. "Make yourself comfortable. Would you like a slice of pie?"

Emmett sat, watching Edna slice an ample piece of apple pie. He was ashamed at the way his mouth watered seeing the crispy crust. Perfect slices of cinnamon sprinkled apples glistened from the sides. When Edna sat the plate in front of him, it took all his willpower not to dig right in.

Edna's eyebrow arched as she handed him a glass of sweet tea. "Now, tell me what you can do for my brother. I know Mac tried all he could to save him. May the man rest in peace."

Edna moved around the kitchen as she spoke, pulling a large glass casserole dish from the refrigerator and setting it on the counter. Emmett watched as she sprinkled a generous layer of cheese over what looked like a chicken and rice mixture. Then she reached for a canister of breadcrumbs. Her hands never stopped working, even as her eyes remained fixed on him, waiting for his answer.

Emmett took a sip of the tea to give himself a moment. "Your brother is dying, Miss Boyd. You know that. I believe him when he says he didn't kill James Whitaker, and I will do all I can to turn over any new evidence I can find."

Edna's eyes narrowed as she spread the breadcrumbs evenly across the top of the casserole. "I've heard about you, Emmett Craig. You're apparently very good at what you do."

Emmett remained quiet. No matter what he did, he couldn't seem to shake the repercussions of his last case.

Silence sat between them until Edna broke the silence. "And why would you believe a man convicted by a jury of his peers?"

"I admired and loved Mr. Mac. He was ... a father figure to me. I believe your brother's case was very close to his heart. If his health hadn't failed him, I know Mr. Mac would still be fighting for your brother. And Mr. Mac entrusted me with his remaining cases. I will do right by him and your brother."

Edna sighed, pausing briefly to wipe her hands on her apron before opening the preheated oven. Heat billowed out as she slid the casserole inside. She set the timer and turned back toward him, her face shiny from the heat. "Mac was a good man. You know, we all grew up together."

She paused and looked out the window for a second. "The last time I saw Mac was a few days before he died. And you're right. He was still fighting for his buddy from school." She turned around and eyed Emmett. "Do you know what he found that had him so anxious?"

He met her gaze steadily. "I'm still searching through the case file. But the evidence against your brother was suspiciously convenient. It was like he wanted to get caught."

"My brother was framed!" Edna huffed. She turned her back to Emmett as she washed her hands at the sink. "James Whitaker was not the easiest man to work with. Me and my sister-in-law, God rest her soul, tried to discourage Darrell from the partnership. But one of my brother's faults is his loyalty. He'd always had a lopsided friendship with that man, even when they were boys."

She dried her hands and moved back to the refrigerator, pulling out lettuce, bell peppers, tomatoes, and cucumbers. As if forgetting he was there, she began methodically washing and chopping the vegetables.

Emmett dived into the pie, sensing from the way Edna chopped the vegetables that she might need a moment. Savoring every bite of the apple pie, he watched as she assembled a salad.

Edna covered the salad bowl and placed it in the fridge. She glanced over at the time before turning her attention back to him. "I'm sorry, Mr. Craig. I'm using up your precious time. Did you enjoy the pie?"

He smiled. "I did. It was delicious. And, Edna, I assure you I plan to revisit what others had to gain from Whitaker's death. I also want to dive into any enemies he may have had. From Mr. Mac's notes, he'd been hunting down

Thad Jenkins. I understand Jenkins was fired from the construction company a week before Whitaker's demise and had threatened to 'make Whitaker pay.'"

Something flickered in Edna's eyes. "Yes, that Jenkins man may have been a problem. But as you know, the cops focused on Darrell from the beginning." She smiled. "You're pretty tenacious, Mr. Craig. I see why Mr. Mac chose you to continue his practice. I got to ask though. What's next for Darrell? My brother may not make it." Her voice cracked, and she looked away, wiping her hands on her apron. "And he can't stay in *that* place."

Emmett had only seen Darrell twice, but he could see the man needed medical help. He hesitated with his response. "When I spoke to Darrell yesterday, he seemed more focused on seeing his daughter. I reached out to Tracey this morning and asked if she could come to South Carolina."

Edna let out a shaky breath. "Oh, my Lord! I tried to obey her wishes. It didn't matter how people treated me, but there were people in this town who weren't kind to Tracey after Darrell was arrested. People she'd known her whole life seemed to turn on her in the worst way. It didn't help that the Whitaker family made sure everyone knew what her father supposedly had done before the trial."

"That's why I'm here. I wasn't in town back then, and I want to understand what we're up against."

"I will try to give you as much detail as I can." Edna removed her apron and placed it across the counter. "Let's leave this hot kitchen."

Emmett followed her into a living room off the kitchen. This one was much less formal than the sitting room area he'd entered at the front of the house. From the photos arranged on the wall above the fireplace and lined up on the mantle, Emmett decided this must be the family's private quarters in the bed-and-breakfast.

His attention was drawn to a photo in the center of the mantle. A woman with caramel skin and large brown eyes gazed back at him from the photo. She held a young boy who appeared to be about two years old in her arms. He pointed. "Tracey and Jayden, I presume?"

Edna smiled, but her eyes were sad. "That picture was taken the Christmas before Tracey moved down to Florida. Jayden is a second grader now. Hard to believe how much he's grown since then."

"She's beautiful," Emmett said, then immediately regretted it. That was not the kind of observation an attorney should make about his client's daughter. "I mean..." he stuttered.

Edna's smile widened. "My niece is beautiful. So nice of you to notice."

He knew he needed to turn away, but he couldn't take his eyes off Tracey's face. Her face was older, but he remembered the younger version. After finding her photo in his yearbook, many memories of hanging out over at the Mac's house flooded his mind.

"I was two years ahead of your niece in school. She was good friends with Charlene McMillan."

Edna chuckled. "Well, you have quite the memory. Tracey and Charlene are still best friends. I guess you did know Mac and his family well."

It was his turn to grin. "I grew up hanging out with the McMillans. Kenny is still a buddy of mine. He saved this skinny white boy on several occasions back in the day."

Edna threw her head back and laughed. "You had your own bodyguard. Kenny had his father's girth, but he got his height from his mother's side of the family. I'm feeling even better now. I see why Mr. Mac chose you to represent my brother. Have a seat over there."

After putting his foot in his mouth, he was glad Edna wasn't ready to throw him out. This couldn't be easy for Edna, having to run a business while her younger brother, dying behind bars was starting over with a new lawyer. He sat on the couch and waited while Edna rummaged through a cabinet. His eyes swung back to the photo of Tracey with her son. Memories of her flooded him. He doubted she would remember him. She clearly didn't know who he was when he'd called this morning.

Of course, no one called him Emmett in school. There had been a variety of names he'd been called instead. Most of them weren't pleasant.

Edna had grabbed a photo album and opened it to a page showing a much younger Darrell Boyd standing proudly in front of a construction office with another man. Both wore hard hats and grinned at whoever had snapped the photo.

"James founded Whitaker Construction in 1995. In the beginning, Darrell worked for him as a foreman. After being there about two years, James made my brother a business proposition to become a partner."

Emmett frowned. "Why did he do that? Seems like the Whitakers would have kept it in the family?"

Edna grunted. "You're thinking like I was when Darrell told me. They'd been friends throughout school. When James married Helen, Darrell was his best man. When Tracey's mother, Judith, died of cancer, Helen brought food every day for a month. Judith and Helen were college roommates."

Emmett commented. "Sounds like a solid friendship between the families."

Edna raised an eyebrow. "Mmm. My brother's friendship always leaned toward James mainly getting his way. Darrell has always been easy going. Did you know my brother wanted to start his own construction company? He must have talked to James about it and tried to get his advice. Next thing, James convinced Darrell that they would be better working together as partners. What I do know, whatever their business disagreements, Darrell would have never hurt James. Never."

Emmett studied Edna's face. She clearly still believed in her brother's innocence. He hated to state the obvious. "But the jury believed the opposite. That Darrell was angry enough to hurt James."

Edna's mouth tightened. "That argument the day before didn't help matters. I was there. Tracey was there. Darrell definitely lost his temper. But he had a right to be angry. James made him believe he was a partner. But James made a decision that excluded Darrell. It had been Darrell's dream to run a construction company. If James hadn't convinced him of this partnership thing, none of this would have happened."

Emmett had to agree. "Tell me more about the bankruptcy."

Edna sucked in a breath. "James wanted to declare bankruptcy after a big client left them holding the bag on a major development. Darrell wanted to find investors, but James had made up his mind."

"Why wouldn't James want to save the company?"

Edna threw up her hands. "I have no idea. It never made any sense."

"Do you know if James had any enemies? Could there have been something else going on for him to want to dissolve the company?"

Edna seemed to consider her words carefully. "James was well-liked, generally speaking. He was the face of the company since he originally founded it, and it held his family's name. Darrell ran the general operations for the company where James was more of the salesperson. I heard he also had a bit of a ruthless business side. Darrell would joke about it sometimes, but I knew it made him uneasy. I'm sure you already know from Mac's files that James was the one who fired Thad Jenkins. But Jenkins openly threatened James *and* Darrell."

Emmett frowned. "And the cops questioned him?"

Edna nodded. "My understanding is that Thad had an alibi. Darrell's main problem was not being able to explain how that paperweight and money got into his truck. He'd parked it out back inside the shed. Anyone could have snuck in there during the night and planted that stuff. We never locked it. But none of it ever made sense. Why would Darrell take money from his own company? That solicitor painted Darrell like a criminal mastermind who tried to cover up murder by making it appear like a burglary gone wrong." She threw up her hands. "I'm sorry. I'm sure you know all of this already."

"It's good to hear your perspective. Edna, I'm going to concentrate on the motion for Darrell's medical transfer first. We need new evidence to appeal, and I imagine even if we had it, there would be some resistance from the family. There still might—"

"Why? They got their conviction! They did my brother wrong."

Emmett sighed. The Whitaker family had a lot of influence here in Beaufort. Already convinced he was responsible, they'd turned on Darrell. Emmett read in Mr. Mac's notes that James's son, Alex, was on the city council now. James's daughter, Rachel, had taken her mother's place coordinating the annual charity gala at the country club.

"I've heard Helen has become a bit of a recluse. Maybe they won't cause a problem, but I'd rather be prepared."

Edna blinked rapidly. "Maybe. I feel bad for Helen. I do. She loved James and hasn't been right since his murder. I hope her children don't interfere. I want my brother to get any treatment he can to extend his life. Or... at least make him comfortable."

Tears swam in her eyes as she gazed at the photo of her niece and great-nephew. "I'm going to reach out to Tracey. I know she's feeling blindsided right now. She's built a new life away from here. It's not going to be easy for her to return."

Emmett followed her gaze to the photograph. He'd noticed Tracey's smile didn't quite reach her eyes, like she was carrying a burden but trying to appear unburdened for her son's sake. He felt bad that he had to tell her the news of her father's illness over the phone.

A beeping sound from the kitchen interrupted his thoughts. "That's my casserole," Edna said, rising from her seat. "Let me just turn it down to keep warm."

Emmett remained seated as Edna bustled back to the kitchen, his eyes still fixed on Tracey's face. He wondered how Tracey would deal with her father's illness. He could relate to her leaving town to make a new life.

That's what he'd done. But his return back home sometimes felt like his biggest mistake.

Chapter 5

Panama City, Florida
Saturday, May 10 at 9:32 a.m. CST

Saturday morning sunlight streamed through the blinds casting striped shadows across Tracey's living room. Jayden sat cross-legged on the floor, eyes glued to *Spidey and His Amazing Friends* playing on the television. His Spider-Man action figure lay forgotten beside him as he watched heroes more his age team up to protect the city.

Tracey sat with her legs curled up under her on the couch. Wrapped in her pink terrycloth robe, she held a mug of ginger tea in her hands. The conversation with Emmett Craig yesterday loomed in her mind. She hadn't slept well, still not sure what to do. Her phone vibrated in her robe's pocket. She pulled it out and checked the caller ID.

Aunt Edna.

"Jayden, I need to take this call. I'll be in my room if you need me, okay?"

Not glancing her way, he responded. "Okay, Mama."

Tracey stepped into her bedroom, slightly closing the door so she could hear Jayden. She took a deep breath and answered.

"Good morning, Auntie."

"Tracey, baby girl." Her aunt's warm voice flooded the line, bringing with it a wave of homesickness that Tracey often experienced.

She sank onto the edge of her bed. "I think I know why you're calling. That lawyer called me yesterday, told me about Daddy."

There was silence on the other end. When Edna finally spoke, her voice was softer. "I'm sorry you had to find out that way. I wanted to tell you myself, but..." She trailed off.

Tracey asked, her voice almost a whisper. "Is he really dying?"

"Yes, baby girl. Stage four colon cancer. " Edna's voice caught. "The prison doctors say maybe six months. I'm hoping it's not too late to get him treatment."

Tracey closed her eyes, a tight knot formed in her throat. Despite everything, the years of anger and hurt, the news pierced her heart.

"When did he find out?"

Edna paused. "He's known since late last year. Your daddy didn't want me to tell you at first. He's proud, you know that. Didn't want your pity."

"What changed?"

"*That* place he's in. Honey, he can't die in there. Your daddy should have never been put in prison." Her aunt remained quiet for a few seconds. With her voice more calm, she continued, "His new lawyer, Emmett Craig, is concentrating on getting a medical transfer."

Emmett Craig.

The name had been tugging at something in Tracey's memory since the lawyer called her. "Craig? His name sounds familiar. Is he from Beaufort?"

"Why, yes. He mentioned he was a few years ahead of you in school. Said he remembered you from when you used to visit with Charlene. He and Kenny are good friends."

Tracey searched her memory. There was a skinny boy with reddish hair who always hung around with Kenny when she visited the Mac house. They'd called him Redd, not Emmett. She remembered him being quiet, stealing glances at her when he thought she wasn't looking.

"I might remember him." Tracey was surprised that she'd recalled this detail from her past life. "Tall and skinny with red hair?"

Her aunt laughed. "That sounds like him. Not quite as skinny now. Apparently Mr. Mac thought highly of Mr.

Craig, left his practice to him. He's young, but I believe he's willing to figure out if there's a chance to clear Darrell's name before..."

Tracey sucked in a breath. "After all these years, he's still claiming he didn't do it?"

"Because he didn't!" Edna yelped. "I've never doubted that, not for a single day."

"You heard how they argued. Daddy threatened James."

"I know what kind of man my brother is," Edna insisted. "People say things in the heat of anger. Your daddy was loyal to that man. He considered James Whitaker a brother. Yes, James's refusal to save their company hurt him, but your daddy is not a killer."

Tracey rubbed her temple, feeling a headache beginning to form. She never wanted to believe her father was a murderer. But sitting in that courtroom, the solicitor had painted a different picture of the man she knew.

"How's little Jayden doing? He looks more like his daddy every day in those pictures you sent."

The sudden shift in topic caught Tracey off guard. Her aunt had always been good at diffusing a tense situation, still calling her baby girl, even though she was now in her thirties. "He has Jordan's smile, that's for sure. Sometimes it catches me off guard. Jayden was sick earlier this week, actually. Had to stay home from school for a couple days."

"Nothing serious, I hope?"

"Just some bug that came with a fever." Tracey hesitated. "My boss was livid that I stayed home with him. She expects me to be at her beck and call 24/7."

"That Regina woman. Yeah, you told me about her." Edna scoffed. "She sounds like a real piece of work."

Tracey sighed. "Yeah. We just landed this big client, a banking association. They're coming in August for a retreat, and the east wing renovations are already behind schedule. Regina was in full panic mode, even though I worked on the presentation from home. Hopefully after Monday, she'll calm down."

Edna said. "Do you think you can come home? Just for a week or two."

"I really don't know. I can't just drop everything. I have a job. Jayden has school. It's not that simple."

"It never is, baby girl. But your daddy's dying. Be transparent with them. Your employer has to show some grace. I know as long as you've worked for them you have to have some sick leave."

Tracey stared at the envelope from her father, still unopened on her dresser. "What would I even say to him?" In her head, her voice sounded like she'd reverted back to being a little girl.

"You don't have to say anything. Darrell will be overjoyed just to see you." Edna's voice softened. "You know I have plenty of space here at Sweetgrass. That boy should see his grandfather too."

"In prison?" Tracey's voice rose. "You want me to take my eight-year-old son to a maximum-security prison?"

"Children can visit with adult supervision." Edna paused. "But that's your decision, of course."

Tracey stood and walked to her bedroom window, gazing out at the street where they'd lived for the past five years. Panama City had never fully felt like home, despite her best efforts. Maybe that had been deliberate on her part.

"I'll think about it," she said finally. "I have to get past this big presentation on Monday."

"Sounds good, baby girl."

Tracey picked up on the relief in her aunt's voice. They chatted for a few more minutes about the bed-and-breakfast before saying their goodbyes. Tracey had loved working at Sweetgrass. She'd gained most of her marketing and hospitality skills there at a young age. It would be good to visit.

At least that part would be good.

Saturday, May 10 at 11:17 a.m. CST

After ending the call with Aunt Edna, Tracey grabbed her MacBook from her bag. She didn't know why, but Emmett Craig's name tugged at her memory. Obviously Mr. Mac trusted the man, and her aunt had renewed vigor about her father's case.

Was Mr. Craig really that good?

She opened a browser and typed his name into the search bar. Several results appeared, including a LinkedIn profile. She clicked on it. A professional headshot loaded onto the screen, and Tracey's breath caught.

She knew him!

That awkward, skinny boy with red hair had grown into a handsome man with intelligent eyes behind stylish frames. His hair had darkened to auburn, and defined cheekbones and a confident smile had replaced the boyish roundness of his face. He looked nothing like the shy boy who used to hang out at the McMillan house.

Tracey had always been curious about him. He stood out as being odd in Mac's boisterous home, yet somehow he fit in. Kenny treated him like a brother and their mother, Mrs. Mac, seemed to adopt every child that showed up at their house including Tracey. She'd spoken to him plenty of times, mostly about teachers and sometimes books.

If she remembered correctly, "Redd" left town right after graduation. She scrolled down to his bio. He'd graduated from law school with honors and had practiced in Atlanta before returning to Beaufort.

She went back to the browser search and found numerous news articles about a controversial case involving a businessman named Preston Langley.

Lawyer secures acquittal in hotly contested murder case.

She clicked on the first headline and scanned the article. Emmett had defended businessman Preston Langley against murder charges, securing his freedom on what appeared to be technical grounds despite substantial evidence. The victim's family had been vocal about their outrage, and public opinion sided with the Sullivan family against Langley.

Tracey sat back, unsettled. It seemed like she remembered some Sullivans growing up. What did it mean for her father that his attorney was known for getting men off on technicalities and with this kind of news coverage? She closed the laptop, not sure if she shared her aunt's trust in Emmett Craig. But he held her father's fate in his hands.

Tracey's eyes were drawn to the envelope on her dresser. When was she going to get the courage to open it? She stood and walked over to the dresser, but before she could grab the letter, a small knock came at her door.

"Mommy?"

She turned quickly toward the door. "Hey, sweetie, come in."

Jayden pushed the door open, his dark eyes, so much like his father's, regarded her curiously. "I'm hungry. Can we have lunch now?"

"Sure! How about grilled cheese?"

Jayden nodded, but didn't move from the doorway. "Who were you talking to?"

"That was Aunt Edna. What do you think about going to visit her?"

He clapped his hands together. "Yeah, that would be great. Auntie has a big house where different people stay, right?"

Tracey smiled. "That's right. She runs a bed-and-breakfast. Kind of like a hotel, but it feels more like a home."

Jayden leaned against the doorframe, fidgeting with the hem of his T-shirt. "I heard you talking about Grandpa."

Tracey's breath caught. Maybe she should have closed the door completely. "You did?"

He nodded solemnly. "You said he's in prison. What did he do?"

Tracey closed her eyes briefly. It wasn't that she'd completely kept Jayden in the dark about his family. She'd kept framed photos of both her parents in the living room and her bedroom, so Jayden would know about her parents. He often stared at the picture of her mom and then at her. Then he'd say, "You look just like her."

That always made Tracey smile and feel sad because her mom wasn't around. So many things about motherhood, and being a woman, she felt like she'd just stumbled through without her mom's guidance. Sure, Aunt Edna was there, but Tracey had been old enough to remember her mother. She also watched her battle breast cancer, which left a lasting effect on her. Since her maternal grandmother suffered the same fate, Tracey remained vigilant in getting her mammograms and doing her self-examinations.

She didn't want to leave Jayden with that hollowed out feeling of missing her, especially since she'd been his only parent most of his life. Tracey kept photos of Jordan in the living room and beside Jayden's bed so he could see his father, who was now in heaven. But the conversation about his grandfather and his imprisonment had been more difficult to discuss. Now her son gazed at her waiting for an answer.

"Come here." She walked over to her bed and sat down.

Jayden crossed the room and climbed up beside her. Tracey put her arm around his small shoulders, drawing him close.

"The police thought he hurt someone very badly, and that's why he's in prison."

"Did he?"

The direct question pierced her, making her skin tingle. She wanted to believe, like her aunt, that her dad would have never lost control and killed James Whitaker. But she'd sat in that courtroom and heard the evidence. Then there was the jury's verdict. All of it had been too much. But now, faced with her son's simple query, she found herself hesitating.

"I don't know, baby."

"Can we go see him? I don't really remember him."

"You were a baby, well, a toddler, the last time you saw him."

"If he's sick, we should visit him. You took care of me when I was sick."

Tracey couldn't argue with her son's logic.

"You're right," she said softly. "We will have to make a lot of plans. You will miss more school."

"That's okay with me." Jayden nodded. "Hey, can I have extra cheese on my sandwich?"

Tracey laughed. "Extra cheese it is."

They headed to the kitchen as Tracey's mind raced. How was she going to break the news to her boss on Monday?

Chapter 6

Beaufort, South Carolina
Sunday, May 11 at 3:12 p.m. EST

Emmett parked beside several other vehicles in the gravel driveway of the McMillan's home. He took a moment to breathe in the familiar scent of barbecue smoke that hung in the air. The main thing that had changed at the modest two-story house since his childhood days was the loss of one of the oak trees.

And Mr. Mac.

Mr. Mac had been strong like an old oak tree. Then the storms of life had toppled them both.

After visiting with Miss Boyd yesterday, he'd spent more time combing through Mr. Mac's files and starting his own notes. Emmett preferred electronic versions to his mentor's old school system. His priority this week was to convince a judge to get Darrell transferred for treatment.

Voices and laughter drifted from the backyard toward Emmett as he climbed out of his car. He removed his tie, tucking it into his pocket and unbuttoned his collar. He meant to stop by the house and change clothes after church. In his excitement, he'd headed straight to the McMillan's home, his mind on the Sunday cookout. He attempted to cook for himself, but ended up ordering takeout most nights.

As he rounded the side of the house, the gathering came into view. Emmett hesitated, taking in the scene. People clustered around picnic tables with plates of food. Children of various ages chased each other across the backyard. Though he was the only white person present, it felt more like coming home.

A booming voice called out. "Redd, what's up, man?"

All Emmett could do was shake his head. That was his name around here to most. Kenny McMillan swaggered across the lawn. At thirty-four, Kenny still had the powerful build of the high school linebacker who'd once protected Emmett from bullies. His broad smile was framed by a neatly trimmed mustache and goatee.

"It's about time you showed your face around here. We missed seeing you a few Sundays now." Kenny clapped him on the back.

Emmett coughed from the impact of his friend's gesture. "Good to see you too, Kenny,"

"Mama's been asking about you."

He'd been summoned this morning by Violet McMillan. Emmett had a feeling he knew why Mr. Mac's widow wanted to see him.

As they crossed the yard, Emmett received warm greetings from familiar faces. He and Kenny climbed the stairs to the back porch. Before they could enter the kitchen, a woman barreled out with a toddler on her hip.

Face framed with box braids redder than his own hair, she stopped and stared at Emmett, her eyes widened. A slow smile spread across her face as she looked him up and down. "Tell me that isn't Redd."

Emmett grinned. "In the flesh! Hey, Charlene. How do you feel becoming an aunt again?"

Charlene laughed. "My brother and sister-in-law can't seem to stop making babies, but I understand them wanting a girl."

Kenny guffawed. "Oh, stop it. She can't wait to be a girl auntie."

Charlene fluttered her eyes. "Well, I have lots to offer."

Emmett blurted before he could think. "Have you spoken to Tracey Boyd recently?"

Charlene glanced at her brother before looking back at him. "No, you know Tracey left town years ago. I visited her in Florida, over a year ago. But it's been a few months since we talked." She tilted her head to the side. "Why?"

"Well, she might be coming back. I remember you two were friends, so I thought I'd mention it."

Charlene's mouth opened wide as if in shock. "Tracey is coming back here. How, and who convinced her to do that?"

Emmett realized he probably shouldn't have brought it up. He didn't know if Mr. Mac had told his family about Darrell's condition before he died.

A few kids raced by the porch yelling. Charlene turned around and shouted at them to stop all the noise. Just like that, she headed down the steps into the yard, saving him from having to explain.

Kenny nudged his arm. "You should head in and say hello to Mama. I know she's going to want to feed you when you get in there."

Emmett was more than happy to oblige Mrs. Mac's wishes.

Violet sat in the kitchen with other female relatives. At fifty-six, her chocolate face remained wrinkle free, but her eyes had lost their usual brightness. Grief had ravaged her face, creating deep, dark circles under her eyes. She and Mr. Mac had only been one year apart in age. They'd known each other all their lives. Even surrounded by her family, without him there, she somehow appeared a little lost.

"Emmett," she extended her arms, a ghost of a smile on her face. Unlike her children, Violet called him by his name instead of his nickname. Her melodic voice had always soothed him.

He embraced her gently, conscious of the other women eyeing him.

She patted his cheek. "Have you been eating? You never seem to gain any weight."

He grinned, already salivating for a plate of food. The Macs cooked enough to ensure everyone had to-go plates. "Mrs. Mac, you know you're the only one who feeds me."

That she did. Violet fixed a heaping plate of barbecue chicken, collard greens, mac and cheese, and two pieces of cornbread glistening with butter. The familiar smells transported him back to his childhood when he'd practically lived at the McMillan home.

Emmett dived into the plate while catching up with Kenny on the back porch.

Kenny asked. "How's that old house coming along? You still trying to fix it up yourself?"

Emmett grimaced, thinking of the home he'd inherited. "Very slow. I want to rip out the wall between the living room and kitchen. I think it would open up the space a lot, but I'm questioning if I can do that on my own."

Kenny gestured with his fork. "Construction's my thing, man."

"I could sure use your help, man." Emmett took a bite of mac and cheese, savoring the taste.

Kenny nodded. "How long has it been since you been back? Over a year, right?"

"Almost two," Emmett corrected. "My dad died two years ago." He stared out at the yard, not focused on anything. His complicated emotions about his father continued to plague him. "We never really patched things up, you know?"

Kenny's face turned somber. "Your dad left you that house though. Once you get it fixed up, it will be a really nice place."

"Yeah. My brother and sister wanted nothing to do with it or Beaufort. Chelsea is happy living in her Atlanta suburb. I don't know what Jake is doing out in L.A." Emmett shrugged. "Sometimes I wonder why I came back at all."

"Because this is home for you. Things should get better for you." Kenny stated. "You got *that* case behind you."

Emmett said nothing. Although he didn't hear any judgment in his friend's voice, his own guilty thoughts still plagued him about his involvement in Langley's non-guilty verdict. All of them had been concerned for him, especially Mr. Mac.

Kenny looked around before leaning forward. "You still feeling okay with the security system?"

Emmett thought about what he should say. He didn't want to worry Kenny. "It's been quiet. But I'm glad you convinced me to put it in. And..." he hesitated, "I appreciate you going with me to get that piece. Never thought I'd own one."

Kenny eyed him. "Better safe than sorry, man. Your neighborhood has always had some weird stuff going on. Though it's gotten better since a lot of them abandoned houses were torn down. Still, you're way out there, off to yourself. Plenty of privacy."

Emmett thought to himself. *Yeah, but people can find me if they want to.*

An uneasy silence settled over them. The family gathered as usual, but Mr. Mac's presence was sorely missed. He glanced at his friend, who'd grown quiet. "How's everyone doing?"

"We're moving forward as best we can." Kenny said matter-of-factly. "You mentioned Tracey. I know you can't tell me anything but I'm guessing you're going to take on Darrell Boyd's case. My dad and Darrell were friends all their lives."

"Edna mentioned that when I went to see her."

"Yeah," Kenny smiled. "Miss Edna is the only one that can rival my mama's cooking. But don't tell Mama I said that."

Emmett chuckled, happy to get past the awkward moment. He had a question for Kenny. "Hey, do you know who your dad used for investigations?"

"You mean private eye stuff? Yeah, Jack Daniels."

Emmett frowned. "Like the drink?"

His friend threw his head back and laughed. "Like the drink, man. But he's good people. Him and my pops played poker. Mr. Jack was a cop for a long time, now he's retired. Mama can probably give you his number."

"Sounds good, man."

Kenny eyed him. "I hope you're not going to be like Pops, working all the time. You're too young for that. We got to get you married. You can't stay in that house all by yourself. You trying to become Bachelor of the Year around here?"

Emmett almost choked with laughter. "Everyone can't have what you have. Anyway, I don't have time to date."

Kenny cocked his head to the side. "Well, I recall you having a crush on a certain cutie pie. Doesn't matter that it was a long time ago, seeing that she's coming back to town and all."

Before Emmett could respond, Violet appeared at the screen door. "Emmett, do you have a minute?" Her tone was casual, but her eyes conveyed something more serious.

"Sure, Mrs. Mac."

Kenny gave him a knowing look. "Careful, she's probably gonna ask why you're not married yet too."

Emmett eyed his friend. Surely he wasn't about to suggest Tracey to him. That wouldn't be feasible at all. He shook his head. Ever since Kenny had settled down, family was all he talked about. Sure, it would be nice to find the woman of his dreams and settle down with two kids and one on the way like his friend.

But work was his only mate at the moment.

Sunday, May 11 at 4:03 p.m. EST

Emmett followed Violet through the house, away from the noise of the gathering. She led him to a door at the end of the hallway, which Emmett realized was Mr. Mac's home office. When she unlocked it and switched on the light, Emmett was struck by how everything remained exactly as it had been when Mr. Mac was alive. Law books still lined the shelves, case files were stacked neatly on the corner of the desk, and the worn leather chair still held the indentation of the man who'd spent countless hours working there.

"I haven't changed anything," Violet said softly, closing the door behind them. "The kids wanted me to clear it out, but I couldn't. Not yet. It hasn't even been six months yet." She ran her fingers along the edge of the desk. "Sometimes I come in here just to sit. Feels like Drew might walk through that door any minute, complaining about Judge Abernathy or Solicitor Jennings."

Emmett smiled. "He had strong opinions about them both."

Violet fingered the cross pendant at her neck. "How's Darrell doing? I saw Edna at church this morning. She mentioned you've taken his case."

"He's not doing well," Emmett responded. "The prison's medical care isn't equipped for his kind of illness."

Violet frowned. "You trying to get him out?"

"I want to get him transferred to a medical facility. But honestly, he seems more concerned about seeing his daughter than getting treatment."

Violet's expression softened. "Poor Tracey. She was still grieving the loss of her son's father, then that happened. Child lost her mama when she was twelve. Might as well say she lost her father too." She shook her head. "Drew and Darrell were good friends too. He said he never understood the friendship between Darrell and James. James always had the upper hand. That one case took Drew under. He gave everything, fighting to save his friend from prison."

"Edna told me the Whitakers made sure everyone knew what Darrell had allegedly done."

"Allegedly," Violet repeated, giving him a significant look. "You know, Drew never believed Darrell killed James Whitaker. Not for a minute."

Drew. Emmett loved how Mrs. Violet had been the only one to call Mr. Mac the shortened version of his first name. It was good to hear how Mr. Mac felt about this case. "I gathered from his notes that he'd thought the evidence—"

"Was convenient," Violet finished for him. She leaned forward, lowering her voice even though the door was closed. "I don't want the children to know this, but I think Drew was getting close to something just before he died."

Emmett felt a chill, and it wasn't because of the room temperature. "What do you mean? You don't think something was wrong with the way Mr. Mac died?"

Violet closed her eyes, wrapping her arms around herself in a hug. "No, nothing like that. Drew's heart had been bad for years. The man was hardheaded, wouldn't listen to the doctor or keep up with his blood pressure medicine."

She paused as if trying to prepare herself for what she was about to reveal. "Something was bothering him those last few weeks. He'd come home late, lock himself in his office for hours. When I asked, he'd just say, 'Better you don't know, Vi.'"

Emmett frowned. "Do you think he found new evidence?"

"I think he found something." Violet looked past him, her eyes on the window behind Mr. Mac's desk. "Those few days before his heart attack, he was unusually quiet. When he got like that, something was on his mind."

Last week, Miss Edna mentioned that Mr. Mac seemed anxious the last time he visited.

Right now, Emmett was concerned about Mrs. Mac, who appeared shaken. "Miss Violet, are you okay?"

She nodded. "I just haven't been able to stop thinking about it. The last time we really talked about it, he said something that's stayed with me all these months. He said, 'I should've looked harder at the Whitakers from the beginning. The way they turned on Darrell so quickly... people with nothing to hide don't act that way.'"

"The Whitakers?" Emmett repeated.

Violet nodded solemnly. "He was fixated on them those last weeks. Said something about financial records that didn't make sense. You know that company that supposedly went bankrupt leaving Darrell and James holding the bag?"

"Okay, that's good. I'll go back and review those files."

Violet hesitated before moving to the desk. She picked up a worn black leather Bible and extracted a folded piece of legal paper tucked inside. "I found this a few weeks ago. I don't know why it wasn't included with the other files. I think Drew got up in the middle of the night to scribble this down and placed it in his Bible. He used to keep a pad of paper on his nightstand."

She handed Emmett the note in Mr. Mac's distinctive handwriting. He read it. Then read it again to be sure of what he was seeing.

Check Whitaker finances.

Langley's connection to Coastal Developments.

Alex knows something.

"I don't know what it means," Violet said softly. "But Drew was convinced there was more to the story than what came out at trial."

Emmett stared at the note. He could feel his heart rate increasing. "Have you shown this to anyone else?"

Violet shook her head. "I figured it was too important."

"Thank you for showing me." Emmett carefully folded the note and tucked it into his pocket. "I still have a lot of files to go through. Mr. Mac enjoyed handwriting his notes."

Violet's face brightened as a small laughed slipped from her. "I told him he had the worst handwriting of anyone I'd ever seen. I guess doctors and lawyers have that in common or something."

He shrugged. "I type out everything when I can."

They both laughed, but then grew quiet.

"Emmett." Her eyes held his with an intensity that made him straighten his posture. "You need to be careful. Drew always thought Darrell was framed, which means if someone else did this, they had the good fortune of covering their tracks. Drew wouldn't want anything happening to you on account of this case. The stress of it... I think it's what finally took him from us."

Mrs. Mac's warnings stayed with him as they returned to the family gathering. But the note in his pocket.

The note haunted him more.

Langley.

God, I don't need that type of connection to this case.

Chapter 7

Monday came too fast. Tracey gripped the laser pointer, trying to appear confident despite the nervous energy rippling through her body. Inside the Morrison conference room, Henry and Regina Morrison, along with two executives from the Southeast Banking Association, focused on the screen behind her.

"As you can see from these renderings, the east wing renovations will create an exclusive retreat space unlike anything else on the Gulf Coast," she explained, clicking to the next slide. A stunning view of what would soon be a luxurious suite with a private balcony overlooking the ocean appeared on the screen. "Each suite will feature custom amenities tailored to executive needs, including dedicated workspaces and high-speed Wi-Fi."

She caught Regina's nod of approval. For once, her boss seemed pleased. Tracey dreaded the woman's reaction when she requested more time off. Throughout the weekend, she'd stared at the letter from her father, still unopened, debating whether it would make things better or worse.

The only confirmation she was making the right decision was Jayden's excitement for the trip. She would need to talk to his teachers. There were still a few weeks of school left before summer vacation.

"Ms. Boyd?"

The question from the Southeast Banking vice president pulled her back to the present. "Yes, Mr. Cunningham?"

Jasper Cunningham leaned forward, his silver hair catching the light from the windows. "These executive suites look impressive, but I'm concerned about the timeline. You mentioned the east wing would be complete by late July. Our annual executive retreat is scheduled for the first week of August. Is there any risk of delay?"

Tracey opened her mouth to respond, but Regina cut in smoothly.

"We've built in a buffer with our contractors, Mr. Cunningham. I can personally guarantee the renovations will be complete with time for a thorough quality inspection before your arrival."

There was no way Regina could make that guarantee. The construction was already behind schedule. But Tracey kept her mouth shut. This was Regina's show.

Cunningham nodded, "That's wonderful."

Tracey moved through the remaining slides on autopilot, discussing dining options, recreational activities, and special event spaces. She was grateful for the last slide and gladly turned it over to her boss.

Regina stood. "We'll have lunch coming for you gentlemen shortly. Then we can discuss the details of your booking."

Henry Morrison had been unusually quiet. "Why don't we do that tour before lunch?"

Regina stood and clapped her hands together like she was about to perform a cheer. "That sounds great."

Tracey resisted the urge to roll her eyes. Regina was being 'extra' energetic today. She hoped the woman remained in good spirits.

Henry turned toward her. "Great job on the presentation, Tracey. Will you be joining us?"

She shook her head. "I need to catch up on a few things in my office."

"Well, we appreciate your work on this proposal." Henry's eyes sparkled. "And I'm glad to hear your son is feeling better."

She smiled. "Thank you, sir." Henry was charming like that, always remembering things you didn't think the CEO would retain. Too bad some of his charm hadn't rubbed off on his daughter.

As soon as they all left the conference room, Tracey's shoulders sagged from exhaustion. A headache had started to brew from all the fake smiling and overselling. It didn't help that her mind was half in South Carolina, imagining what it would be like to face her father after all these years. Did his new lawyer really think he could find any new evidence when so much time had passed?

In the beginning, Tracey believed in her father's innocence. He'd always been a gentle man. But she'd witnessed her father's intense anger the day before his partner's murder. She and many others had witnessed the fight that turned physical. It was the nail in the coffin from the prosecutor.

Tracey sat staring at her computer monitor, not really seeing the designs she was supposed to review from the graphic designer.

She'd lost track of time when Regina strutted into her office without knocking. "We did it. This booking will cover at least half the renovation costs. My father is ecstatic."

"That's great." Tracey managed. Even after all her hard work and having to put up with Regina, the successful presentation didn't concern her. They'd clearly over-promised, but Tracey had bigger concerns now.

"I need to speak with you about something important."

Regina's smile faltered a bit. "Sure, what's wrong? The presentation was perfect."

This woman! Tracey took a deep breath before diving in. "I need to request some time off."

"Time off?" Regina's eyebrow arched in confusion. "Tracey, we just landed Southeast Banking. There's a mountain of work to do, and we have to finish the renovations on time."

"I know, and I wouldn't ask if it wasn't important. My father is dying. I need to return home... back to South Carolina."

Regina's expression shifted from irritation to uncomfortable surprise. "Oh. I... You've never talked about your father."

"We're not that close. But he has cancer."

"I see." Regina stood rigidly still and began twisting her hands. "How much time are you thinking?"

Tracey had researched her options over the weekend. "I'm not sure. At least a week, possibly two. I have accrued plenty of sick leave, and I believe this would qualify for FMLA if necessary."

Regina frowned. "Two weeks? Tracey, that's not possible right now. We have the contracts to finalize, the website to update with the new renderings—"

"Is everything all right, ladies?" Henry's voice interrupted as he entered Tracey's office. Tracey was surprised to see him. She didn't recall him ever coming to her office before.

Regina turned to her father. "Tracey is asking for two weeks off. Right in the middle of our busiest season with the Southeast Banking contract just landed."

Henry's bushy eyebrows rose as he looked to Tracey. "That doesn't sound like our Tracey. Must be something important."

"It is, Mr. Morrison. My father is very ill. Terminal cancer. I need to go to South Carolina to... to see him before..." She couldn't finish the sentence.

Henry's expression softened immediately. "Of course you do, my dear. Family comes first. Always."

"But the marketing materials—" Regina began.

"Tracey has good plans that folks can follow." Henry interrupted gently. He turned toward her. "If you can, and only if it's not inconvenient, maybe you can handle some tasks remotely, like you did while your son was sick."

"Absolutely, Mr. Morrison."

He glanced over at his daughter. "Tracey's been with us for five years, Regina. She's been a hard worker." He turned back to Tracey. "Take whatever time you need."

Praise God! Relief washed over her. "Thank you, Mr. Morrison. I can complete the Southeast Banking contract before I leave, and I'll be available by phone and email if anything urgent comes up."

"Don't worry about that now," Henry said. "When do you plan to leave?"

"Well, I need to talk to my son's teacher. But I'd like to leave Saturday morning."

Henry nodded. "I see. Well, if you need any help, just say the word. My sister Lauren was very fond of you."

The kindness in his voice nearly broke Tracey's composure. Before her retirement, Lauren Morrison had indeed been a mentor and friend during Tracey's first years at the Morrison. Tracey hadn't realized Lauren was experiencing early onset Alzheimer's during her last few months. They'd joked about her forgetfulness. Now her former boss stayed in the memory care unit of a comfortable nursing home.

"Thank you," she managed, blinking back sudden tears. "I appreciate your understanding."

Regina forced a smile. "Yes, well, family matters are important. Just make sure you brief Mia and Javier on anything urgent before you go."

Tracey nodded. It would be no problem keeping in touch with Mia. Javier, the graphic designer, would be overwhelmed by Regina, but Tracey would make sure he could reach her. "I'll prepare detailed notes and set up a shared folder with all the current projects."

"Good." Regina glanced at her father and left Tracey's office.

Henry lingered, his kind eyes studying Tracey's face. "I didn't know about your father's situation, Tracey. I'm very sorry."

She admitted. "Our relationship is ... complicated."

Henry nodded. "Family usually is. But at the end of the day, they're still family." He paused. "If you need to extend your stay, don't worry about Regina. Just let me know directly."

After Henry left, Tracey took a shuddering breath. His kind offer brought more tears to her eyes. She hadn't expected this to be easy and thanked God for Henry stepping in to head off his daughter. Tracey knew it would only be for a while. Regina would find a way to hound her as she'd done the two days Jayden was sick.

Now, Tracey needed to make travel plans.

She was really going to do this. This trip would require more than just seeing her father again. Tracey would have to face the people responsible for her fleeing her beloved hometown.

Chapter 8

Beaufort, South Carolina
Monday, May 12 at 9:52 a.m. EST

Emmett hadn't slept well since yesterday's family gathering. Violet's concerns were now his. Last night he stared at the note, wondering how Mr. Mac came across these leads? He hadn't been able to fully comb through all of Mr. Mac's notes and files. The last thing he expected was to see the name Langley again.

He was able to locate the private detective, Jack Daniels, who had great pride in his name. They agreed to meet tonight. Filing the motion for the medical transfer request was Emmett's first priority this morning.

Darrell Boyd's stage four colon cancer required treatment beyond what Lieber Correctional could provide. The prison doctor provided detailed documentation of Darrell's deteriorating condition and the facility's limited resources for cancer treatment. Edna had called him yesterday confirming her niece would arrive in Beaufort by the weekend. Despite any concerns, moving forward with the motion seemed promising.

The drive to the courthouse took less than fifteen minutes. Beaufort's oak-lined streets were a far cry from the congested traffic he'd grown accustomed to in Atlanta. After he parked, Emmett checked his reflection in the rearview mirror, adjusting his tie. He'd chosen his best suit today, knowing appearances mattered in a small town where everyone knew everyone's business.

Inside the courthouse, Emmett joined the short line at the security checkpoint. He emptied his pockets into a small plastic tray—keys, phone, loose change—before placing his briefcase on the conveyor belt. The metal detector beeped softly as he walked through, causing the older security guard to wave his wand around Emmett's belt buckle.

"You're good." the guard said with a nod.

"Thank you." Emmett replied as he collected his belongings.

Footsteps echoing off the high ceilings and polished floors, he made his way down the corridor. Though the courthouse had undergone renovations a few years back, it still clung proudly to its past. Portraits of long-gone judges hung in frames, their stern gazes seemed to follow him as he passed.

In the clerk's office, a handful of paralegals and attorneys milled about, exchanging paperwork and quiet conversation. When he reached the counter, he placed the motion before the clerk, a woman whose decades of service were etched into the fine lines around her eyes.

"Filing for Judge Abernathy," he said to the clerk. Her glasses hung from a beaded chain around her neck.

She glanced at the document, then up at Emmett. "For Darrell Boyd?" Her eyebrows rose slightly.

Emmett suddenly felt on edge. "Yes, ma'am. A medical transfer request."

The clerk's lips pursed. "I'll make sure the judge gets it." Her tone was neutral, but her eyes stated her bias.

"Thank you." He forced a smile and turned to leave. If he hurried, he could make it to the hospital to meet with Dr. Patel, the oncologist who had agreed to review Darrell's case. The doctor had a full schedule but had squeezed in a fifteen-minute consultation as a favor to Emmett.

Emmett rounded the corner toward the courthouse exit and almost collided with a man.

"I'm sorry—" he stopped short when he recognized who stood before him.

Alex Whitaker, impeccably dressed in a navy suit, looked equally surprised. He'd grown into his square jaw, and his blue eyes were even more penetrating. Emmett used to hate to see Alex coming when he was younger. The spoiled rich boy, now a man, had been terrorizing.

"Well, if it isn't Emmett Craig." Alex's voice was smooth. "Heard you were back in town."

Emmett forced a smile. "Yes, I've been back awhile."

When Emmett was a freshman, Alex had been a senior. He was the stereotypical blonde, blue-eyed jock who excelled on the high school football and baseball teams. Combining his athletic prowess with his wealthy family, Alex had been a main attraction to many adolescent girls. He'd heard via Kenny that Alex, once a Homecoming King, had married his Homecoming Queen, Lucy Barnes, after they'd both graduated from college.

Emmett was no longer the skinny kid who feared seeing this older boy and his friends coming down the hallway. Though Alex still had a lot more pounds on him, he faced him eye-to-eye. Emmett imagined the suit Alex wore cost more than a lot of valuable materials he needed to renovate his house.

Alex certainly hadn't lost his signature smirk. "I heard you were a lawyer. I bet your old man would've been proud of you. He was a hard worker...when he wanted to be."

Emmett did his best not to flinch at the subtle jab. Typical Alex. Always with an insult.

Many people worked for the Whitakers back in the day, including his father. But Richard Craig's love for liquor or beer, depending on his mood, often interfered with his work ethic. His father's drunken actions also made Emmett an easy target for ridicule from people like Alex. Emmett straightened his back, the muscles in his cheek tightened with the fake smile he'd been attempting to wear. He was a lawyer, he knew how to play the game.

Alex's eyes flickered to Emmett's briefcase. "Working on anything interesting these days?"

"Keeping busy. And you? I hear you're on the city council."

Alex smiled. "Just doing my civic duty. Following in Dad's footsteps, you might say."

An uncomfortable silence stretched between them. *Was this just a coincidence meeting him here?*

"I should get going," Emmett said, stepping to the side. "I have an appointment to keep."

Alex didn't move. "You know, I went to Mr. McMillan's funeral. He was a bit of a legend around here, so I had to give my respects. I heard through the grapevine you've taken over his practice. Including his... older cases."

Emmett could feel his body tense. "Mr. Mac was my mentor."

Alex nodded slowly. "He was a good man. Stubborn, though. Couldn't let go of lost causes." His eyes hardened. "I hope you're more practical."

"I believe everyone deserves proper representation."

"Ah," Alex's eyes narrowed. "I bet you're here about Boyd. I heard he was sick."

Emmett stared back at the man like he was some snake about to bite.

"The man murdered my father." Alex's voice remained level, but there was steel beneath it. "He bashed his head in and a jury convicted him. That man should never see any kind of freedom for the rest of his life."

"I'm aware of the details."

"Then you should know Darrell Boyd deserves whatever comes to him." Alex took a step closer, lowering his voice. "We've all moved on. My mother. My sister. The community. I heard what you did to get Preston Langley off. Made quite a name for yourself around here. That will not happen for Boyd."

Emmett gritted his teeth. "This is a separate case. And since you seem to know so much, then you know I'm filing a motion for a medical transfer. That doesn't equal freedom. The man has terminal cancer."

"Good." The word felt like a slap.

Emmett frowned at the venom radiating from Alex Whitaker. "Even a condemned man deserves humane treatment."

Alex's face reddened. "You know what wasn't humane? Finding my father with his head bashed in. Having to identify his body. Watching my mother collapse at the funeral. She's never been the same." He stepped back, composing himself. "But, hey, you're just doing your job, right? Isn't that what you told the press after Langley?"

"That's what I was doing."

Alex let out a sharp laugh. "Getting criminals off. What a job!"

Emmett bristled, but remained quiet. He remembered part of Mr. Mac's scratched note.

Alex knows something.

Why was Alex really here?

"I have a meeting with Judge Abernathy in ten minutes." Alex made a show of checking his watch. "He's an old family friend. I know he will see the futility of this request."

Emmett kept his face blank as Alex walked away. Despite the warm air, he felt a chill. In that instance, Alex's entire demeanor reminded him of his former client, Langley. Bending the rules and making deals to meet their demands.

This could not be happening!

He glanced around, hoping no one had been watching his run-in with Alex. Emmett wondered if Mr. Mac had run-ins with any of the Whitakers the past few years. He couldn't imagine anyone facing down Mr. Mac the way Alex just did to him. But then again, Alex had confessed to attending Mr. Mac's funeral, which seemed odd.

If Darrell Boyd was innocent, as Mr. Mac believed, then someone else murdered James Whitaker seven years ago. And that someone had allowed an innocent man to go to prison. Who would do such a thing? Destroying not only a man, but letting those repercussions affect the man's family. His own daughter had to flee this place.

Violet's warning settled in Emmett's mind as he headed toward his car.

Was this the stress Mr. Mac felt? Emmett became more convinced that he had to find out who really killed James Whitaker.

Monday, May 12 at 7:42 p.m. EST

Emmett pulled into the gravel parking lot of The Blue Heron, a diner at the edge of town. The blue neon sign flickered to life as the sun continued to make its descent for the night. He scanned the lot, noting the mix of pickup trucks and modest cars before cutting the engine. The salty air hit his nostril as he stepped out of the car. Not too far away, he could hear water lapping against the pier.

His earlier meeting with Dr. Patel at Beaufort Memorial had gone well. The oncologist had reviewed Darrell's medical records and agreed about the urgency for proper treatment. Patel's credentials were impeccable, and Emmett thought his diagnosis would be accepted by Judge Abernathy. At least he hoped.

The confrontation with Alex had rattled him more than he cared to admit. Not just because the man purposely tried to interfere with Darrell's medical transfer, but because Mr. Mac's note cast suspicion. Did Alex have anything to do with his father's death? Did the Whitakers have a connection to Langley?

I should've looked harder at the Whitakers from the beginning.

That's what Mrs. Mac remembered as some of her husband's last words before he died. What had Mr. Mac stumbled upon? Emmett was here at the diner to meet with the P.I. who had worked with Mr. Mac and saw what he knew.

The diner smelled of greasy burgers and seafood. Monday nights weren't busy, and only a handful of patrons occupied the serving counter and worn wooden booths. Even though Emmett had never met him before, he easily spotted a man he believed to be the infamous Jack Daniels. A tall man with dark skin sat alone in a corner booth. As Emmett approached, he saw the man leaning over a plate of burger and fries. The man glanced up observing Emmett as he drew closer.

Jack wiped his face with the napkin and sat back. "Mr. Craig, I presume."

"Yes, sir."

Jack held out a large hand. "Have a seat, young man."

Emmett slid into the booth opposite him. Jack reminded him of Mr. Mac in some ways. Both men were of the same era, sporting short-cropped gray hair. But Jack's straight posture spoke of a military and police background. His face was weathered, but his eyes were sharp and observant.

"Thanks for meeting with me."

Jack shrugged. "Been expecting your call to be honest. Not sure why you took so long."

A server approached. "Can I get you something, sir?"

Emmett grabbed a menu from the end of the table. He was tempted by Jack's burger and fries. That's what he really wanted. But lately, he'd been eating unhealthy and hadn't worked out in a week or so, so he opted for the shrimp po'boy instead. It wasn't exactly healthy with the thick crusty bread, but the grilled seafood would be better than a greasy burger. Besides, the po'boy was a Blue Heron specialty, and he needed the brain fuel tonight.

When the server left, he turned his attention back to Jack. "I talked to Mrs. Violet this past weekend. She mentioned Mr. Mac had been working on something." Emmett wasn't ready to share the note yet. He wanted to see what Jack had to offer.

The man stuffed fries in his mouth and passed a manila folder across the table toward Emmett. "This was the last job I did for Mac."

Emmett decided to keep the folder closed until the server returned with his food. "What exactly did you find?"

Jack took a long sip of soda. "Whitaker Construction was bleeding money long before James was killed, and not just from *that* bankrupt client everyone talked about." He pointed to the folder. "There are bank statements inside that show someone was systematically draining the company funds for at least a year. Classic embezzlement pattern."

The server arrived with Emmett's food. He really wanted to open the folder, but he was famished. He dug into his side salad before inquiring. "Was it James?"

"That was my first thought too," Jack said. "But Mac and I came to the conclusion it had to be someone else. If James discovered the embezzler, that was the perfect motive to kill him."

Emmett's mind whirled back to Mr. Mac's note. "What about Alex Whitaker? James brought him into the company around that time, right? I had a run-in with him earlier today. He's gunning to keep Darrell from getting medical care."

Jack's eyebrow rose. "Now that's interesting. Let's hold that thought for a minute." He opened the folder and pulled out a paper with letterhead. "This company, Coastal Developments, LLC approached Whitaker Construction about a resort project. Big money. The kind of contract that could save a failing company."

He slid across a grainy surveillance photo. James Whitaker was shaking hands with a tall man in an expensive suit, his back to the camera. "This was taken about three weeks before James was killed."

Emmett's blood ran cold. Something about the stance, the build, and the way the man held his head up seemed too familiar. "Do you know who that is?"

Jack shook his head. "Not with certainty. Poor angle from the surveillance camera. But based on the timeframe and the business registration documents I pulled..." Jack extracted another paper from the folder. "Coastal Developments was owned by Preston Langley."

The name hung in the air between them. Emmett felt his throat tighten, and his appetite disappeared.

Jack's eyes sharpened. "You know him?"

Emmett hesitated, then nodded. "He was my most recent client."

Understanding dawned on Jack's weathered face. "The murder case? I heard about that. You're the one who got him acquitted."

"On a technicality." The admission tasted bitter in Emmett's mouth. "The evidence was collected improperly. They had a search warrant for the house, but not for Langley's boathouse."

Jack leaned back, studying him. "Well, that's one heck of a coincidence, isn't it? You defend a man for murdering his business partner, then take on the case of another man convicted of a similar crime."

"It's not a coincidence." Emmett frowned. "Mr. Mac thought it was best to leave his cases with me. I imagine there is someone higher up than both of us at work here."

Jack laughed. "They say God has a sense of humor." He gazed at Emmett intently. "You might cross paths with the man you helped walk free."

Emmett stared at the photo, his mind racing. "If Langley was involved with James Whitaker, and their business relationship went south, like it did with Bobby Sullivan, then you're right. I would have to—"

Jack finished. "Prove it! Then you might can get an innocent man out of prison."

A *dying man.*

Emmet swallowed. "How solid is this connection?"

Jack shrugged. "Not enough for court. But enough to keep digging. Mac was convinced there was more to find." His expression darkened. "Then he died."

"What if the murderer was closer, like someone in the family?"

Jack eyed him. "You were talking about the son earlier. Alex Whitaker?"

"Someone on the inside did the embezzling. Darrell managed the job sites, but he didn't deal with investors. That was all James. None of this financial stuff came up at the trial."

"You're right. Mac always hated that he didn't have enough to give the jury reasonable doubt. He thought everything moved too fast with that case. One reason why he had a bone to pick with Judge Abernathy and Solicitor Jennings." Jack gathered the documents, returning them to the folder. "I'll keep digging into Langley and Coastal Developments. And if you want me to, I can look into Alex. See if I can find a money trail."

"It may not lead to anything, but it's a path Mr. Mac was pursuing."

"Mac was a good man. One of the few who always did the right thing, even when it cost him." Jack's expression softened slightly. "He spoke highly of you too, kid. Said you had the brains and the heart to be a great lawyer as long as you didn't get jaded."

Emmett felt a lump in his throat. "I'm trying to live up to that. I feel like I disappointed him with defending Langley."

"Well," Jack said, sliding out of the booth, "this is a good start to redeem yourself. Word of advice. The older I get, the more I lean on prayer. It keeps your moral compass in the right direction."

Emmett grinned. "That definitely sounds like something Mr. Mac would have said to me."

Jack extended a calloused hand, which Emmett shook firmly. "I'll be in touch when I have something more concrete."

Emmett took care of their bill and left a hefty tip. As he headed out to his car, the cool night air did little to clear his troubled thoughts.

But he had leads now.

Instinctively, something told him to look up.

Blinding headlights bore down on him as an engine roared to life. A pickup truck barreled across the parking lot, heading straight for him. Emmett's body reacted before his mind could process. He dove to the side, landing hard on the asphalt. The truck's tires screeched as the driver tore past him and out onto the highway.

"Oh, my God!" A woman cried out from behind him. "Are you hurt? Should I call an ambulance?"

Emmett pushed himself up. His hands were scraped and bloodied. Seeing his suit pants torn at the knee, he softly swore under his breath.

"Sir? Are you okay?"

He looked over to the female voice speaking to him. An older woman peered at him, her eyes wide behind thick-framed cat-eye glasses.

"I'm fine," Emmett managed. "Just... lost my footing. I should have been looking before I started walking."

She eyed him and then looked out to the street. "Seemed like that truck came out of nowhere. People should be more careful. He could have hit me."

Emmett brushed gravel from his palms, smearing blood across his hands. "Did you see the driver?"

The woman clutched her leather handbag closer to the front of her body. "It looked like a large man wearing a baseball hat."

Emmett's instincts were on high alert. He doubted the woman was in any danger but felt the driver intended to...to what? Scare him? Or run him over?

"Oh, look at your hands," she said. "At least let me get you some napkins."

Not having the heart to refuse her, Emmett waited until she came back, still trying to process what happened. Was that the same truck that was outside his house? The lights were so bright he couldn't see anyone behind the driver's seat. But from his good Samaritan's recollection, it was a large man. That could be anyone.

Arnold Sullivan is a large man who drives a pickup, and he has been stalking me.

That he was sure of.

He graciously thanked the woman for her help and walked her to her car which was parked on the same row as his BMW.

He climbed inside his car and sat, still processing as his body tried to slow the spike of adrenaline. Langley's trial was six months ago, but the victim's brother, if that was him, seemed to be escalating.

But why was Emmett the target when he'd only been doing his job? If he'd known what he did now, he would have never taken Langley as a client.

Chapter 9

Panama City, Florida
Saturday, May 17 at 7:05 a.m. CST

Tracey loaded their luggage into the trunk during the early hours of Saturday morning. She'd debated booking a short flight into Savannah, or even Charleston, but the cost of plane tickets made her stomach twist. Besides, driving would give her time to think. To prepare.

A sleepy Jayden climbed into his booster seat, clutching his Spider-Man backpack. Her son slept the first ninety minutes. He ate one of the granola snacks she'd packed and kept bringing items from his backpack. She smiled as she glanced at him in the mirror. Jayden settled on a Marvel coloring book for a while, then he read one of his assigned books from school and finally moved on to his tablet.

Tracey was happy they'd been able to work out an e-learning plan with Jayden's teacher. She hoped they would be back for him to participate in the end-of-school activities like field day, but she wasn't sure. Ironically, she had the same uncertainty five years ago when driving from Beaufort into the unknown.

"How much longer, Mom?" Jayden's voice piped up from the back seat.

She grinned and glanced at the dashboard clock. It was nearly 8:15 a.m. When she looked at Google Maps on her phone, it jolted her. It was an hour ahead. At some point, they'd crossed from central time to eastern time.

"We have a lot more road to cover, sweetie," she said. "We'll stop soon and stretch, maybe grab an early lunch. How does that sound?"

Jayden sighed and leaned his head back with a dramatic eye roll. "This is taking forever."

"I know. Do you need to use the bathroom?"

"No, I'm good." Suddenly energized, he asked, "Can I get nuggets?"

She chuckled. "Yes, we will find you some nuggets."

Tracey had set a small goal to make it out of Florida before stopping for a real break. Nerves on edge all week, she hadn't even grabbed a cup of coffee. She was driving on pure adrenaline.

As Tracey drew closer to the Georgia state line, her mind drifted to Emmett. She'd had plenty of time to think about what she discovered online. The Preston Langley case seemed like a big deal. Had he returned to Beaufort just to take that case? Some of what she read concerned her. Did he genuinely believe in her father's innocence the way Aunt Edna did?

Jayden's voice pulled her from her thoughts. "Mom, I'm hungry."

"We'll be stopping to get some food and take a break from the car soon. You can hold on a while longer, can't you?"

Grumbles from the back seat met her ears.

Tracey's mind slipped back into her earlier thoughts. She resolved to be cautious around Emmett, not really understanding his true intentions. Her priority had to be protecting Jayden and herself, something she'd worked hard to do over the past five years.

About thirty minutes later, they pulled into a Chick-fil-A, just before crossing into Georgia. The parking lot was busy but manageable. Jayden had his seat unbuckled and had climbed out of his booster seat before she could stretch her legs good.

"Hold on," she yelled.

After they ordered, Jayden claimed a booth by the window, where he gazed out while dipping his nuggets into the Chick-fil-A sauce. Tracey had just taken a bite of her grilled chicken sandwich when her phone buzzed with a missed call. Aunt Edna.

She tapped to call back as she took a sip of sweet tea.

"Well, hey, baby girl," Edna answered on the second ring, her voice warm and familiar. "Where y'all at now?"

"Just stopped for lunch," Tracey said. "We're about to cross into Georgia."

"Oh good. You all left real early. Sound like you're making good time. How's my boy doing?"

Tracey grinned. "Gobbling up chicken nuggets. We should be there by five or six, depending on traffic near Savannah."

"Well, I've got your old room ready for Jayden and your favorite peach cobbler cooling right now. Take your time and drive safe."

"Thanks, Auntie. We're looking forward to it."

Jayden stared at her phone. "Will there be other kids at Aunt E's house?"

Tracey shook her head. "It's not just a house, it's a bed-and-breakfast. Remember, I told you people stay there when they're traveling? I don't think there will be kids right now, but there's a big backyard where you can play."

"Are you excited to see your dad?" Jayden asked, dipping a nugget into a puddle of sauce.

The question caught her off guard. "I... it's complicated, buddy."

"Because he's in jail?"

She nodded slowly. "Partly. And because I haven't seen him in a very long time."

"I'm excited to see him," Jayden declared with a simple childlike certainty. "And does Aunt E still make those cookies you told me about?"

Tracey smiled. "Auntie is always baking good stuff to eat."

"Mmmm, I can't wait to try."

After lunch, Jayden succumbed to sleep, his head lolling against the side of his booster seat. Tracey drove in silence, watching the landscape change from the flat coastal plains to the gentle rolling hills of South Carolina's Lowcountry. Familiar landmarks appeared, and memories flooded back.

The sign welcoming them to Beaufort triggered a physical reaction. She took a deep breath, reminding herself why she was here. Her father was dying. Whatever had happened between them, she couldn't let him go without seeing him.

Driving through town, Tracey's grip tightened on the steering wheel when they passed the old basketball court where Jordan had spent countless afternoons. She'd watched him from the bleachers so many times, never imagining their story would end so abruptly, leaving her to raise their son alone.

Her hometown appeared both familiar and strange as they drove along. Moss-draped oaks, she'd always loved, still lined the streets, while unfamiliar new businesses now occupied spaces where she remembered others.

Sweetgrass B&B welcomed her as she drew near, but unlike its guests, this had been her home. Tears sprang to her eyes, seeing the palmettos and hydrangeas that had required effort from her entire family. Her aunt, mother, and father spent many springs planting and maintaining the garden. After pulling into the gravel driveway, she cut the engine but remained seated, both hands still gripping the wheel for a long moment.

Memories of going to the hardware store and helping her aunt pick out the paint color for the rocking chairs flooded her. Her dad, already sentenced, was serving time at Lieber Correctional. Tracey knew Aunt Edna had thought up the DIY project more as a distraction for both of them.

The chairs rocked in the afternoon breeze, their blue color a bit faded now. Tracey's eyes went to her aunt's prized ferns hanging in baskets from the porch ceiling. There seemed to be even more plants than she recalled. And the garden outside the horseshoe window had also grown. They'd planted some of those bulbs when her mama was still alive.

How did her aunt maintain all this?

The front door swung open, and there was Aunt Edna with a hand on her hip. Her aunt shielded her eyes from the sun, but her wide smile welcomed them home.

"Jayden, wake up. We're here." Tracey reached back and gently shook her son's knee.

He stirred, blinking sleepily, and stretched his arms. "Finally!" As if he'd been zapped fully awake, Jayden yelled. "Whoa, it's like a mansion!"

Tracey laughed. "Not quite, but it's pretty big." The house had been in their family for decades. Her aunt, dad and two deceased sisters had grown up here. After her grandmother died, Aunt Edna along with her parents had transformed the home into a modern bed-and-breakfast, keeping the bottom half of the house for family.

"You made it!" Edna shouted.

Jayden was already unbuckling his seatbelt. "That's Aunt E. Can I go say hi?"

"Of course," Tracey said. She'd tried to keep her aunt connected to Jayden via Facetime calls, but it wasn't the same as being in person. It broke Tracey's heart sometimes that Jayden was growing up away from all the people she loved. Edna had been there for her after her mother died.

Edna opened her arms wide, catching Jayden in a bear hug. "Look at you! All grown up! Last time I saw you, you were just a little thing."

Tracey approached slowly as unexpected tears flooded her eyes. When Edna turned her gaze toward her, Tracey saw her eyes were also shining with unshed tears.

"Baby girl," Edna said softly, opening one arm while keeping the other around Jayden. "Come here."

Tracey stepped into her aunt's embrace, inhaling the familiar scent of vanilla and cinnamon that always seemed to cling to her. For a moment, she was a child again, safe and protected.

"Let me look at you," Edna said, stepping back and holding Tracey at arm's length. "Still as beautiful as ever, but you look tired, chile."

Tracey smiled despite the exhaustion that tugged at her eyes. "It was a long drive."

"Well, you're home now. Come on inside. I've got sweet tea cooling and your rooms are ready."

Jayden bounced up and down. "Can I see the whole house? Mom said it's huge inside!"

Edna laughed. "How about I give you the grand tour while your mama brings in your bags?"

They disappeared inside, and Tracey returned to the car for their luggage. The weight of being back in Beaufort settled over her shoulders like a heavy cloak.

Was it still home after all these years?

She carried their suitcases up the porch steps, pausing to look at the street. A couple walked hand in hand on the sidewalk. An older man worked in his garden across the way. Normal, everyday life continued on as if she'd never left. As if her world had never been shattered here.

Inside, the bed-and-breakfast smelled of a home-cooked meal, something sweet, and furniture polish. The entryway opened into a sitting room with comfortable-looking furniture and bookshelves lining the walls. To the right, a curved staircase led to the second floor where guests stayed.

Edna's voice drifted from deeper in the house, accompanied by Jayden's excited questions. Tracey followed the sound to find them in the kitchen, where her son was already perched on a stool at the island, a glass of milk and a cookie in front of him.

"I was just telling Jayden about his room," Edna said. "It's where your mama used to stay when she was a little girl." She glanced at Tracey. "You have your parent's room."

"That's fine," Tracey replied. Mama still wanted to work at the bed-and-breakfast, even during her chemo treatments. This had been Tracey's home growing up, even after her mother died. Her dad opted to stay here since Aunt Edna was around to help watch over Tracey.

"Well, take your things up and get settled. Dinner will be ready soon."

Upstairs, Tracey showed Jayden to his room first. Her old room had changed over the years. She could see in her mind where posters of Chris Brown, Usher and Destiny's Child had been pinned on the lavender walls. Her aunt had the walls painted a pastel blue now and a nautical-themed quilt was draped over the full-sized bed. The desk and chair where she'd sat to do homework was still near the window. It occurred to her that the room felt just right for a little boy. Almost like her aunt had been planning this room for Jayden.

"This is awesome!" Jayden exclaimed, immediately investigating the bookshelf stocked with children's books.

"I'm glad you like it. My room is just across the hall if you need me." Tracey set his suitcase on the bed. "Want to unpack your things now or explore some more?"

"Explore!" he declared without hesitation.

She laughed. "Okay, but stay inside or in the backyard, and don't bother any guests if you see them."

Jayden hustled back down the stairs to the kitchen. Tracey crossed the hall to her own room. Her parent's room. It was exactly as she remembered. Her mama picked the lavender wall color and white antique furniture. She'd missed this room, especially the cozy window seat overlooking the street. Her Mama loved sitting on that bench. Sometimes she would sit there at her feet while her mama braided her hair.

Tracey sat on the edge of the bed, suddenly overwhelmed. Edna had refreshed the bedding and curtains over the years, but she imagined seeing her Mama getting ready for church in front of the oval-shaped full length mirror. Her father mulling over what tie to wear, while Mama fussed that they would be late for church.

There was quite a bit of sadness tied to this house. How many nights had she cried herself to sleep across the hall in her old room? After Mama died? After Jayden's father died? After her father's conviction? How many mornings had she awakened hoping it had all been a nightmare?

Pushing the memories aside, she crossed to the window and pulled back the curtain. She gazed into the oak trees in the background, listening to the sound of Jayden's voice. Hopefully, he stayed in the backyard.

A navy blue BMW pulled into the driveway, catching her attention. Was this one of the bed-and-breakfast guests? Tracey watched as a tall, slender man stepped out with a briefcase in hand. He was dressed casually in a white polo shirt and dark blue jeans. Something about his posture seemed familiar. When he looked up toward the house, she glimpsed a handsome face behind dark-framed glasses. The sunlight shone on reddish-brown hair.

Panic seized her body when she saw Jayden run toward the stranger. Her son knew not to approach strangers. What was he doing? They'd barely been in Beaufort an hour and her mama bear instincts had already kicked in.

She hurried downstairs, wondering why Emmett had shown up now.

Chapter 10

Beaufort, South Carolina
Saturday, May 17 at 5:48 p.m. EST

Emmett knew Tracey and her son had just arrived after a long drive from Florida. The last thing he wanted was to overwhelm her, but time wasn't a luxury Darrell Boyd had. Judge Abernathy had granted the motion for Darrell's medical evaluation, but getting him transferred to the hospital facility would require more than just legal paperwork. The judge wanted assurance that the family would cover any additional costs not absorbed by the state.

A flash of movement caught his eye and he stopped. A small boy raced across the lawn, arms outstretched like airplane wings. Jayden, he assumed, noticing the boy's resemblance to the photos Edna had shown him. He was smaller than Emmett had expected for an eight-year-old.

The boy spotted him and changed course, heading straight toward him.

"Hi!" the boy called out, skidding to a stop a few feet away. "Are you staying here too?"

Emmett crouched down, bringing himself eye level with the child. "No, I'm just visiting. My name is Emmett. You must be Jayden."

The boy's eyes widened. "How do you know my name?"

"I'm a friend of your great-aunt Edna," he explained. "She told me you were coming to visit."

"We drove all the way from Florida," Jayden announced, bouncing on his feet. "It took forever!"

Emmett chuckled at the boy's enthusiasm. He imagined that was a long time to be in the back seat of a car.

"Jayden!"

Emmett looked up to see a woman hurrying across the lawn toward them. Even from a distance, he recognized Tracey. He stood up, smoothing his shirt as she approached. Her caramel-toned skin glowed in the late afternoon sun, and her dark hair had been pulled back in a simple ponytail. She actually looked more like he'd remembered her from school. Though her eyes appeared weary, her face still looked young. She had been a sophomore his senior year, which made her around thirty-two years old.

"It's good to see you, Tracey." Emmett said, "I'm Emmett Craig."

Her eyes flashed with recognition at his name, followed immediately by a guarded expression.

"Mr. Craig," she said, her voice cool.

He quickly tried to explain his arrival. "Your aunt mentioned you'd be arriving today."

Tracey placed a protective hand on Jayden's shoulder. "Jayden, why don't you go see if Aunt Edna needs help with anything?"

"But I want to stay outside." Jayden protested. "Hey, Mister, do you like Spider-Man?" Jayden did a pose as if he was shooting a spider web at him.

Emmett chuckled and threw up his hands pretending to fend off the spider webs. "I love Spider-Man. He's one of my favorite superheroes."

Jayden grinned, "Me too. I'm going to find Aunt E."

The boy ran for the porch, slamming the screen door behind him.

Tracey frowned. "Looks like you scraped your hands."

He cringed, thinking about his near miss last night. "I took a bad tumble on asphalt."

She continued to look at his hands before looking up at his face. "I just got here. Can't this wait until Monday?"

"I understand, but there are some developments in your father's case that can't wait. And I thought you should know about them right away, so you'll be prepared since things are happening on Monday."

"On Monday!" Her shoulders slumped in exhaustion. "Fine. Let's go inside."

Edna was waiting on the porch as they approached. Emmett didn't know why, but he felt nervous under the older woman's gaze. Probably because of the knowing glance she gave him. He had made a fool of himself when he caught sight of Tracey in the photo last week.

"You've reacquainted yourself with Tracey, I see." Her tone remained light, but her eyes were sharp with assessment.

Emmett grinned. "Yes, ma'am. I hope you don't mind me stopping by like this."

"Not at all. I told you she'd be arriving today, didn't I?" Was that a hint of mischief in Edna's smile, or could that have been his imagination?

Jayden bounced up and down beside his great aunt. "Hey, Mister. I forgot your name."

Emmett chuckled, tickled by Jayden's energy. "Mr. Craig."

"Yeah, that's right." Jayden jumped up and down. "Mr. Craig likes Spider-Man too."

"Does he now?" Edna raised an eyebrow at Emmett. "Well, I was just about to make a fresh batch of chocolate chip cookies. Want to help me with the dough?"

"Yes!" Jayden pumped his fist in the air.

Edna turned to Tracey. "You two can talk in the family room. No guests are booked until tomorrow, so you'll have privacy."

Tracey nodded, though Emmett detected reluctance in her posture. He knew his timing was bad, but he needed Tracey to sign-off on papers and be available for court on Monday if she was needed.

She led him to the same comfortable sitting room in the back part of the house. He hadn't noticed the large horseshoe windows that looked out onto the garden the last time he was here.

"Please sit down." Tracey gestured to the armchair while taking a seat on the couch.

Emmett set his briefcase beside him before sitting in the chair. "I appreciate you meeting with me so soon after your arrival. I know the timing isn't ideal."

"Nothing about this situation is ideal, Mr. Craig."

"Emmett, please."

She hesitated for a moment and then said. "Emmett."

He opened his briefcase and removed a folder. "I filed a motion for your father's medical transfer. The hearing with Judge Abernathy will be on Monday."

A flicker of surprise crossed her face. "This is all moving fast, but why the hearing?"

"Your father's condition warranted expedited review. However, there's a catch." He passed her a document from the folder. "The judge wants assurance that the family will handle any costs beyond what the Department of Corrections can't cover."

A wrinkle formed in her forehead as she scanned the document. "How much are we talking about?"

"It depends on the treatment your father receives and how long he remains in the hospital. The state will cover basic care, but any specialized treatments and certain medications may not be covered."

"I don't have that kind of money."

"No worries. Your aunt mentioned she could help, and there are some medical assistance programs we can apply for as well." Emmett leaned forward, meeting her eyes. "The important thing is getting him proper medical care as soon as possible. His condition is deteriorating rapidly."

Tracey set the paper aside. "When will he be transferred?"

"That's the other reason I wanted to see you today. If you can sign these consent forms as his next of kin, we can have him moved in about a week."

"That soon?"

"Yes." Emmett hesitated, then added, "He's asked to see you, Tracey. Before he's transferred, if possible."

"Okay." She looked away. The afternoon light streamed through the window across her face. In that moment, with her eyes slightly lowered, he suspected she was attempting to hide her emotions.

He hated to tell her, but there could be trouble on Monday, and it was best to prepare her now. "There's something else. The Whitaker family is aware of the motion.

Alex Whitaker confronted me at the courthouse earlier this week."

Her head snapped back toward him, her eyes blazing. "Alex has always been a bully. What did he say?"

Emmett knew that from personal experience. "Nothing directly threatening, but the message was clear. He doesn't want your father released. I haven't moved legally on anything but the motion, but he appeared afraid that the case would be reexamined. I understand Mr. Mac was working to do that before he died."

Tracey frowned. "Did Mr. Mac find anything new for an appeal?"

Emmett considered his words carefully. "Your father has always maintained his innocence. Mr. Mac believed him. I've been slowly reviewing the case files and Mr. Mac's extensive notes. I'm prepared to investigate further. I know it's what your aunt wants."

Tracey shook her head. "Mr. Mac and my aunt believed what they wanted, but that jury saw something different."

"Juries can be wrong, Tracey," Emmett said quietly, "especially when influenced by public opinion and a powerful local family."

A flash of anger crossed her face. "Mr. Mac tried to have the trial moved from the county. Lord knows, the Whitakers made sure everyone thought my father was guilty long before the trial started."

"I'd like to hear more about that, if you're willing to talk about it. Your perspective on what happened back then could be invaluable."

Tracey shook her head. "I'm not sure what I can tell you that would help. I wasn't at the crime scene. I didn't see what happened."

"But you knew both your father and James Whitaker. You were present during the argument the day before the murder according to the trial transcripts."

She stiffened. "Yes."

"Would you describe their relationship to me? Not just that day but in general."

Tracey crossed her arms over her chest. "They'd been friends since they were young. My mom was friends with Helen. Alex and Rachel were always much older than me, so I never really got to know them like my parents and their parents knew each other. To be honest, the Whitaker kids were snobby to me. But I liked Helen. She was nice to me after my mom died, always checking in and bringing me things." Her voice grew softer. "I really felt bad for her. Helen took my mom's death hard."

"But your father continued to be friends with the Whitakers. Being a partner in the business."

Tracey huffed. "Some partnership! The business was failing. Their biggest client went bankrupt leaving them with huge expenses and no way to cover them. James wanted to declare bankruptcy and move on. He made decisions without including my dad." She shook her head. "My dad couldn't accept that. He was convinced they could find a way to save the business."

"Enough to kill his partner over it?"

Tracey blinked hard. "My father rarely showed a temper, but he was angry that day, angrier than I'd ever seen him. They both said things. But murder? I still have a hard time wrapping my head around it. I felt like after the dust settled, my dad would have accepted it. You know my dad was more concerned about putting their employees out of work."

Emmett thought it was interesting she wasn't totally convinced of her father's innocence like Edna, but she wasn't certain of his guilt either. Tracey knew there was goodness in her father. He wondered about that argument between James and Darrell. But there had to be something else. Why else would Tracey leave and not talk to her father all these years?

Emmett implored. "Well, anything you can remember about that time might help."

She moved to the edge of the couch. "I'll try. But I want to see my father first. It's only right that I talk to him before digging all this up again."

"Of course. If you're comfortable signing these documents today, I can file them first thing Monday morning."

Emmett passed her the consent forms and a pen. Their fingers briefly touched as she reached out to take the pen from his hand. He swallowed, surprised by the brief contact.

With her head bent scanning each of the papers, Emmett found himself watching her before he caught himself.

"Okay," she said after signing on each line and returning the forms. She examined his face as if waiting for him to tell her the next step.

Act like a professional, man!

Emmett cleared his throat. "If all goes well, I can arrange for you to visit your father at Lieber before the transfer at the end of the week."

She nodded. "I'd like that."

"What about Jayden?" he asked. "Will he be going with you?"

Tracey sighed. "I don't think prison is the right place for him to see his grandfather. Maybe after he's transferred."

Emmett nodded, tucking the signed forms back into his briefcase. "He seems like a great kid."

Her lips stretched into a curve, her dimples making an appearance. "He is. The best thing in my life."

He'd been curious about her life, in particular about Jayden's father. He remembered Jordan Harris had been phenomenal on the basketball court in high school. Many were surprised when the star athlete didn't continue his career. Tracey and Jordan had been high school sweethearts and apparently, their relationship continued, producing a son. Emmett wondered why they'd never married. Maybe they were planning too when Jordan died. His heart broke for her when he learned all that happened just a few months before Tracey's father was arrested and charged with second degree murder.

Despite it all, Tracey had prevailed. Emmett remembered Tracey being really smart in school. Never nerdy like him, though, she had been too cute for that stigma. But he often ran into her in the library checking out books, and they'd talked.

From the brief time he'd been in her presence today, he sensed she was a strong woman. She'd left this town and made a life for herself. He'd done the same. Now they both were back. Well, Tracey would be here for a little while.

"Will you be visiting anyone else while you're in town?" he asked, closing his briefcase.

Tracey shrugged. "It's been so long, I'm not sure anyone would even want to see me."

"I saw Charlene McMillan at her family's house this past Sunday. I mentioned you might come back to town. Weren't you two best friends?"

"Yes, we've kept in touch." She lifted an eyebrow. "Do they still call you Redd?"

His eyes widened at her using his nickname. He hadn't expected her to remember, but a warm glow spread through his chest. "I'm surprised you recognized me after all these years."

Her smile turned shy. "I didn't at first, when you called. It wasn't until I talked to my aunt." She studied him like she was really seeing him, not as her dad's lawyer, but as the teenage boy she once knew. "Your hair isn't as red."

He was pretty sure his face had turned visibly red. "It's darkened the older I've gotten. More of a dark reddish brown now." He grabbed his briefcase and stood. "I should let you rest. It's been a long day for you, and I've given you a lot to process."

She walked him to the door. At the threshold, she hesitated. "Do you believe my father is innocent?"

Emmett met her gaze. "I believe there's more to the story than what came out at the trial. And I believe your father deserves a chance to set things right."

She looked thoughtful for a moment. "Do I need to go to the courthouse on Monday? I mean, is this going to be like the trial?"

He sighed. "It's more of a hearing. But, yes, if you can, it would be good to have you there."

Her smile disappeared, and she grew somber again. "I read about your trial last fall. We're not going to have any trouble with the media are we?"

That figures! What did he expect?

He was a new lawyer for her dad. Of course, she would check him out. Emmett did his best to offer her an honest response. "It's not the way I'd like to work, but your father was convicted of killing a prominent member of this town.

And... I got a reputation from my last case. I'm sorry. I can't make any promises that requesting your father's medical transfer won't draw public interest."

"Of course." She crossed her arms. "Well, you're obviously good at your job."

"Have a good evening." That was all he could manage after her statement. He didn't think she was trying to insult him, but somehow her statement hadn't felt like a compliment. He walked to his car, feeling her eyes on him as he went. Though she'd recognized him from their shared childhood encounters, she was a mother. The way she came outside to protect her son, he knew he'd have to work extra hard to earn her trust.

Even Darrell and Edna hadn't truly believed he could take on the job like Mr. Mac had.

He would do his best for his client and his family, but Emmett had a sinking feeling there would be some bumps in the road.

Part Two

The Homecoming

Chapter 11

Sweetgrass Bed & Breakfast
Sunday, May 18 at 10:07 a.m. EST

Tracey touched the small gold cross. The necklace that used to belong to her mother sparkled above the neckline of the golden yellow dress she'd selected to wear today. While staring at herself in the full length mirror, she pictured her mama's face.

Tracey had inherited her mama's complexion and dark, slightly slanted brown eyes. Her dimples came from her dad. When she was a little girl, she liked to touch his face, but sometimes it was covered with a beard, hiding deep dimples.

She wrapped a matching golden yellow band around her hair to keep it from going full afro once she stepped outside in the humidity. It was also a hairstyle her mother wore. Tracey used to bother her mama about getting a relaxer, so she could wear her hair straight and long, but her mother wanted her to be proud of her curls.

Raising Jayden alone, Tracey decided to forego visits to the beauty salon, opting to keep her hair natural. Most days, she kept her curls braided or twisted in an updo or just wore a ponytail.

She headed across the hallway to check on Jayden. "Almost ready?"

"Do we have to go? I don't know this church. None of my friends are there." Jayden whined and then tugged at the collar of his button-down shirt.

Tracey kneeled to straighten his tie. "It's a different church, but God is still going to be there. And we don't want to make Auntie feel bad, do we? We can visit her church with her while we're here."

He eyed his mother. "Do you know the people at Aunt E's church? Do those people know Grandpa?"

Jayden had always been an inquisitive child, but his last question caught Tracey off guard. "Some of them might."

Jayden nodded. "Are you nervous too?"

Out of the mouths of babes.

Her son's perceptiveness never failed to amaze her. It was like God was using him to get her attention or let her know he sees how she feels. "I'm a little nervous about seeing people I haven't seen in a long time. But we'll be fine." She touched his nose. "God is good."

Jayden clapped his hands. "All the time."

Edna was waiting for them downstairs in a purple suit and matching hat, the brim shaded her eyes. Her smile brightened at the sight of them. "Don't you two look nice? Tracey, my, my, chile. You look like your mama this morning."

"Thank you, Aunt Edna."

Aunt Edna reached out for Jayden's hand, who stepped up and grabbed it. "We'd better get going. I like to get there early enough for a good seat."

Tracey groaned inwardly. That meant her aunt was going to strut them right up to the front of the church.

The drive to Second Baptist was pretty short. As they approached the white church with its soaring steeple, Tracey felt her stomach tighten. This had been her church growing up. She'd been baptized and attended youth group here.

Second Baptist was also where she sat staring at her mother's casket, barely hearing the pastor drone on about her life, and where she'd sat beside her father every Sunday morning after her mother's death. The last time she was here hadn't been pleasant. She'd left before the service even started.

Now, familiar faces in the parking lot turned as they climbed out of Edna's car. Conversations paused mid-sentence. Smiles froze. Tracey felt the weight of their stares as she guided Jayden toward the entrance.

Why did her aunt still attend this church? Of course, her aunt was made of something entirely different. She'd never cared what people said about her and continued to run her bed-and-breakfast even as people said disparaging things about her brother. Tracey marveled at her aunt's inner strength. Something she felt sorely lacking in herself.

"Edna!" A woman in her sixties approached, arms outstretched. "Tracey, you look so good. And is this little Jayden? My, how you've grown up, child."

Tracey searched her memory for the woman's name. The memory that unfolded wasn't a good one. Anita Mason was the kind of woman you needed to be wary about. She was all charm, seeking to extract information that she could later pass along to her gossip train.

Tracey summoned a smile. "Mrs. Mason, it's good to see you."

"We've missed you around here." The older woman's smile seemed genuine, but Tracey caught her aunt's slight headshake. They needed to move on quickly from Mrs. Mason. If people didn't know Tracey was in town, they'd know soon enough from this busybody.

Inside, the church was the same as Tracey remembered. Edna led them to her usual spot, fourth row from the front, right side. As they settled in, Tracey didn't know how she felt. The pews felt familiar and foreign to her brain at the same time. As long as she stared straight ahead, at least she wouldn't see anyone.

A younger preacher had replaced Pastor Williams, who'd retired. The young man's sermon on forgiveness felt painfully relevant. Though Tracey tried to keep her eyes forward, throughout the service, she could feel eyes on her. Whenever she turned sideways, she'd catch a few people staring at her or making whispered comments behind raised hands.

She'd been gone five years, and nothing had changed.

By the time they returned to Sweetgrass, Tracey felt drained.

"You okay?" Edna asked as they entered the house.

Tracey shook her head. "That was a lot. How do you do it?"

Edna grabbed her hands. "Baby girl, people have short memories for the good and long ones for the bad. I don't have time to worry about what other people think. I go to worship God. Now, you go get comfortable. Dinner will be ready soon."

The thought of dinner shifted her mood. She couldn't help but feel excited. Aunt Edna stayed whipping up food in the kitchen. Tracey and Jayden scurried to their rooms to change and returned to serving dishes filled with fried chicken, collard greens, mac and cheese and cornbread.

They finished the meal with slices of sweet potato pie topped with a dollop of whipped cream, and Jayden proclaimed. "This is the best dessert ever."

"Well, I'm glad to hear that." Edna laughed as she stood and started gathering dishes. "Tracey, I hope you don't mind helping me finish up the blue room for my guests.

It's an older couple coming down from up north. I just have a few more things to do in there before their five o'clock check-in."

Tracey stood and grabbed her plate from the table. "Absolutely! I was wondering how you get it all done by yourself."

"Oh, well, bookings are pretty slow during the winter. I have some loyal executives who like to stay when they're in town. But when my busy season starts, I've been relying on some young women. But I haven't found anyone yet for the summer."

Tracey frowned. "Bookings are going to pick up in a few weeks with Memorial Day approaching. I hope you find someone soon, Aunt Edna. You don't need to be running this place by yourself."

Edna propped her hands on her hips. "Chile, I'm not worried. God always makes a way. I trust him."

Tracey found it soothing to fall back into the familiar routine of changing linens. The blue room was aptly named with its pale blue walls and deeper blue curtains framing the windows that overlooked the garden in the front yard.

She added branded water bottles to the bedside tables. Putting the Sweetgrass B&B logo sticker onto water bottles had been her idea a long time ago. It delighted her to see Aunt Edna had expanded the branding with the white monogrammed towels. In the supply closet, she found handmade lavender soap from one of the shops in town.

This was the part of the hospitality world that she missed. She loved marketing for the Morrison to appeal to new and returning guests. But Sweetgrass was where it all started for her.

She was placing the towels in the bathroom of the blue room when she heard raised voices downstairs. Frowning, she listened. The sound of Jayden's name made her blood run cold. Abandoning the towels, Tracey hurried downstairs toward the commotion. As she reached the bottom of the stairs, she froze.

Standing in the foyer, arguing with Edna, were Lydia and Diane Harris. Jayden's paternal grandmother and aunt.

"We have every right to see him," Lydia said. Her voice carrying through the house. "He's our blood."

Edna stood with her hands on her hips. "Tracey just got to town yesterday. If you want to see Jayden, wait until she's ready."

"Ready." Diane scoffed. "She ran off to Florida with him and didn't say a word to us."

Tracey stepped forward, her heart hammering against her ribs. "And you know why I did that."

Sunday, May 18 at 2:43 p.m. EST

Three heads turned simultaneously as she approached them. Lydia Harris straightened, her gaze cold as it swept over Tracey. Fifty-nine and tall, Lydia towered over Aunt Edna. Her deep chocolate skin barely had a wrinkle. "We heard you were back. I came to see my grandson."

Tracey didn't hold back her heavy sigh. This was bound to happen. The thought occurred to her as soon as they ran into that busybody at church this morning. Mrs. Mason and Lydia were good friends. Still, Tracey asked anyway, "How did you even know I was here?"

Diane, five years older than Tracey and bearing a strong resemblance to her late younger brother, folded her arms across her chest. "It's a small town. Word travels fast."

Tracey uttered a silent prayer to keep her head despite the simmering anger. "You can't just show up here unannounced. Jayden is playing outside. This isn't an appropriate time."

Lydia retorted. "Five years, Tracey. Five years without seeing him grow up."

The accusation stung. Tracey wished she had prepared herself for this confrontation. But that would have been impossible. The Harris family had made her life unbearable after Jordan's death, using her father's arrest and conviction to attempt to gain custody of Jayden.

Keeping her voice low, Tracey reminded them. "You were the ones who tried to take him from me. You called me unfit because of what my father was accused of doing. As if murder was hereditary."

"We were concerned," Diane insisted. "You were grieving Jordan, and then your father—"

Tracey cut in. "My father's situation had nothing to do with my ability to parent my son."

Lydia's expression hardened. "You weren't the only one grieving. Jordan was my son. My only son. And you took his child away where we couldn't even see him."

The pain in the older woman's voice was genuine, and for a moment, Tracey's anger faltered. Jordan Harris had been the only man she'd ever loved. Despite her desire for marriage, Jordan was never in a hurry. To the disappointment of her father, Tracey had gotten pregnant. But she never once regretted having Jayden.

Tracey was deep in the throes of grief when her father was arrested for James Whitaker's murder just months later.

Lydia accused Tracey of being emotionally unstable and incapable of providing a proper home for Jayden, using her father's arrest and subsequent conviction as an excuse to petition the court for custody. All because Tracey tried to protect her son. Wanting to keep her little boy close, she'd refused to have Jayden spend time at Lydia's house. Like most people in the small town, Lydia also believed Tracey's father murdered James. There was no way Tracey was going to allow Jayden's mind to be poisoned against his grandfather. He was way too young.

When the judge ruled in Tracey's favor, she'd accepted the writing on the wall. She had to leave this place.

The Whitaker family.

The Harris family.

They'd all lashed out because of their grief. Tracey hadn't deserved the treatment and couldn't leave fast enough when she got the job offer in Panama City. Starting fresh where no one knew her as the daughter of a convicted murderer saved her sanity.

"I did what I had to do to protect me and my son." Tracey's voice was steadier now. "You were hurting. I was hurting. And you pushed the knife in even harder."

Tracey's words lingered in silence.

Diane crossed her arms. "So you still have no intentions of letting us in Jayden's life? You're just here because your father is dying?"

How did they know that? Did everyone know about her father's illness before she did? Before Tracey could respond, the back door opened, and Jayden's voice called out.

"Mom? Aunt E? Can I have a snack?"

He appeared in the doorway to the foyer, stopping short when he saw the strangers. His eyes widened with curiosity.

"Jordan," Lydia breathed, one hand rising to her throat.

Tracey moved to her son's side, placing a protective arm around his shoulders. "His name is Jayden. Sweetie, this is your father's mother and sister. Your grandmother Lydia and your aunt Diane."

Jayden looked up at her, then back at the women. He spoke in a low voice. "My dad's family?"

Lydia stepped forward slowly. "Yes, I'm your daddy's mama." Her voice cracked slightly. "You look just like him when he was your age."

Jayden straightened. "Mom says that too. Do you have pictures of him when he was a kid? I have a picture of him in my room."

"Oh, we got lots of pictures," Lydia said. She glanced at Tracey before breaking into a small smile. "We have a lot of stories about your dad too."

Tracey felt Jayden's excitement building and knew she couldn't send these women away, not without disappointing her son, who had so few connections to his father.

"Why don't we all sit down," she suggested, looking to her aunt for support. "In the family room, not out here."

Edna nodded, though her eyes remained wary. She gave Tracey a look as if to say she hoped she knew what she was doing.

As Lydia passed by her, Tracey stated quietly. "I won't keep him from knowing his father's family, but it has to be on my terms."

Lydia eyed her. "I have always wanted what's best for my grandson."

Tracey stared at the woman's back as she entered the family room. She tried to keep her emotions calm, but she knew she would never trust this woman with her son.

Jayden, oblivious to the tension between the adults, soaked up stories of his father's childhood, laughing at tales of Jordan's misadventures and studying the photos Lydia had in her purse.

When Jayden left to use the bathroom, Diane turned to Tracey. "You've done a good job with him."

The compliment bristled, but she managed to say, "Thank you."

"How long will you be staying in Beaufort?" Lydia asked.

"I'm not sure," Tracey admitted. "I took two weeks off work, but it depends on my father's condition."

Lydia nodded slowly. "We'd like to see more of Jayden while you're here. Maybe he could come spend an afternoon with us? The house is still the same. His father's room is still there."

Tracey felt her defenses rise. "I don't know. We've only been here a day, and I'm taking him to see my father sometime this week."

"You're taking him to the prison?" Diane stated, her eyebrows raised.

"My father is being transferred to a medical facility. He wants to see his grandson."

Lydia's lips thinned. "A child his age shouldn't be exposed to stuff like that."

Before Tracey could respond, Jayden returned. He was full of questions about what sports his father liked, what his favorite food was, and whether he was good at math.

Lydia told him proudly. "Your daddy was something special."

Jordan had been special. Tracey had been loyal to him since high school. She thought for sure when Jayden came along that their son would settle Jordan down. Instead, they'd grown apart. The last time she'd seen him, she'd been so angry. It wasn't the first time she'd found out about his cheating. He was so nonchalant about it, gaslighting her into believing she was being paranoid. Too clingy.

She'd had enough and told him not to come back.

He didn't. He was gone forever.

Edna stepped inside the family room and announced, "I'm sorry to have to do this, but we have guests arriving shortly."

Jayden looked up at Tracey. "Can I see them again?"

"Of course," Tracey answered. "We'll arrange something before we leave town."

Lydia and Diane took turns hugging Jayden. Both women left without looking at Tracey. A cloud lifted off her shoulders once they left the driveway. But it didn't last long.

Seeing his grandmother and aunt had affected Jayden's mood. "I know he's in heaven, but I want to know more about my dad."

The plea in his voice pierced Tracey's heart. She'd told Jayden about his father as often as she could. They did special things on Jordan's birthday, five days prior to Jayden's.

"I know you do," she said gently. "He's not here with us where we can see him, but he's watching over you."

Less than forty-eight hours in town, and Tracey was feeling worn down. Tomorrow morning, when she met Emmett at the courthouse, it was bound to get worse.

Chapter 12

Emmett watched Tracey approach after finishing with the courthouse security checkpoint. She wore a charcoal pencil skirt and cream blouse that looked crisp despite the humid morning. She stopped in front of him, her fingers nervously twisting the strap of her purse.

She smelled heavenly. He had to catch himself from inhaling her. "Good morning," he said.

She gave him a small smile. "Good morning, Redd. Uh... Sorry, I just noticed how red your hair still looks when the sunlight hits it from that window."

He didn't care what she called him. The awkward teenager inside him was flattered she'd caught that detail.

She waved her hands. "I'm babbling. I haven't been in this courthouse since..."

He cringed inside as they started down the hallway. "I'm sorry. I know this must be hard. I didn't think about the fact that you were at your father's trial."

"Every day," she confirmed. "My aunt and I sat right behind my father watching the jurors' faces as they listened to the prosecution paint him as a cold-blooded killer."

"I promise this shouldn't take too long today. We should be in and out."

Out of the corner of his eye, he caught people in the hallway. He stopped walking mid-stride.

Tracey followed his gaze, and her body tensed. "What are they doing here? This is just a medical transfer hearing."

Alex and his sister Rachel stood outside the court doors talking to the county solicitor, Paul Jennings.

Emmett had expected this, especially after his run-in with Alex last week here at the courthouse. But he really wished they'd stayed away.

Tracey sucked in a breath. "This doesn't feel right."

Emmett turned his body in front of her to block her view. "You don't need to engage with them."

Before the Whitakers noticed them, a courthouse clerk approached. "Mr. Craig? Judge Abernathy will see you in his chambers before the hearing. I can take you to him."

The clerk took off. Unfortunately, they would have to pass the Whitaker siblings to get to the judge's chambers.

Tracey looked at Emmett, her arms folded in front of her. "Do we have to go this way? I don't know if I can do this."

She was a few inches shorter than him, and despite his slim build, it seemed like he towered over her. Though he was her father's attorney, he felt the need to protect her.

"We can do this. If they say anything, I will handle it. Come on, we have to catch up with the clerk."

Emmett shielded Tracey as they walked by. As if on cue, Alex turned to glare at them both with his piercing blue eyes. Emmett thought it best not to acknowledge them and murmured to Tracey to keep going. Though he wasn't touching her, he was close enough to visibly see the stiffness in her gait. He expected her to avert her eyes, but she didn't. She stared right back at the Whitakers with her own piercing gaze.

Tracey had some steel in her. When they were safely around the corner, she released a shaky breath.

He touched her shoulder. "Are you okay?"

She pursed her lips. "No, I'm not. They got some nerve. I know they lost their father, but I did too. It's like I'm losing my dad all over again. After all this time, after a jury convicted him, they're still not satisfied."

He realized his hands were on her shoulder, but she didn't seem to mind. With some reluctance, he dropped his hand. "We're going to do what we can for your father. Nothing, not even the Whitakers, will stop this." For his sake, he hoped things went well today. The last thing he wanted to do was disappoint Tracey. He knew it couldn't be easy coming back here, dealing with her father's illness. Having to deal with the Whitakers didn't help.

Judge Abernathy's chambers were tucked at the end of a long hallway, away from the public areas of the courthouse. The clerk knocked once before opening the door and ushering them inside.

Judge William Abernathy was a Beaufort institution. His white hair and round glasses gave him a grandfatherly appearance, but Emmett was familiar with the man's razor sharp assessments. Knowing that Alex had reached out to the man as a family friend, he hoped the judge would do his due diligence and be fair. Mr. Mac had often mentioned to him that Abernathy had been in his position for so long that the man could be unjust.

Judge Abernathy glanced up from the papers on his desk, studying them over the rims of his glasses. "Mr. Craig, good to see you again. And this must be Ms. Boyd." He rose, extending his hand first to Emmett, then to Tracey. "Please, sit down."

Once they were settled, the judge leaned back in his chair, pushing his glasses closer to his face as if that would help him see them better. "I wanted to speak with you privately before we proceed. I understand the Whitaker family is in attendance today."

"Yes, Your Honor. We saw them outside the courtroom. I'm not sure why they need to be here."

Judge Abernathy's steepled his hands under his chin. "They've filed an objection to the medical transfer request."

"On what grounds?" The statement came out a bit more forcefully than Emmett intended, but this wasn't right. The Whitakers had gotten their justice.

Abernathy leaned forward, placing his hands on the desk. "They argue that the medical facility offers less security than the prison, creating potential for escape. They also contend that state resources shouldn't be used to provide care beyond what's available at the correctional facility."

Tracey spoke up. "A dying man is not a security risk."

Judge Abernathy studied her for a long moment. "I'm sorry, Ms. Boyd. I know this must be hard on you, but the solicitor will make that argument in court. I wanted you to be prepared."

"We appreciate that, Your Honor," Emmett said. "But with all due respect, neither argument holds water legally. The Eighth Amendment protection against cruel and unusual punishment has been consistently interpreted to include adequate medical care for inmates."

"I'm well aware of the legalities, Mr. Craig." A hint of amusement crossed the judge's face. "What concerns me is the timing of this request. I know nothing officially has been opened, but am I wrong in thinking you have some interest in the original case?"

Emmett tensed. "Your Honor, as you know I inherited this case from Andrew McMillan. Being the new counsel, I feel obligated to explore all legal avenues available to my client."

"I'm sure you do, Mr. Craig." The judge shuffled some papers on his desk. "But let's be clear that today's hearing is solely about the medical transfer. Any investigation into the original conviction will require separate proceedings."

"Of course."

Judge Abernathy stood indicating their private meeting was finished. "We'll reconvene in Courtroom B in fifteen minutes. I suggest you prepare your client for what might be a contentious hearing, Mr. Craig."

As they exited the chambers, Emmett guided Tracey to a quiet alcove. "I'm sorry. This will be more stressful than it needed to be. I don't know why the Whitakers feel the need to object to the medical transfer."

Tracey squared her shoulders. "Let's get this over with."

Emmett gave her a short nod, admiring her strength.

Then he steeled himself for battle.

Monday, May 19 at 10:00 a.m. EST
The courtroom was already half-full when they entered, mostly with lawyers and clerks waiting for other

cases. The Whitaker siblings had claimed seats in the front row, their presence drawing curious glances from others in the room. Emmett noted with concern that several local reporters were present as well.

"The *Beaufort Gazette* is here." Emmett spoke in a low tone.

Tracey let out a heavy sigh. "That means everyone who doesn't already know about my father's illness will find out."

They took their places at the defendant's table.

Solicitor Jennings was already at the prosecution table, sorting through documents with brisk efficiency. In his early forties, with sharp features and sharper suits, he had a brusque reputation that Emmett had witnessed firsthand with the Langley case last fall. He had no doubt the solicitor would make this difficult on purpose.

"Jennings," Emmett greeted him as they passed.

The solicitor looked up and offered a professional nod. "Craig, I was surprised to see this on the docket."

"Medical necessity."

"So you say." Jenning's gaze shifted to Tracey. "Ms. Boyd?"

Before Tracey could respond, the bailiff called the court to order, and Judge Abernathy entered. Everyone stood for the judge and then settled back into their seats. Emmett could feel Tracey's tension beside him. He scribbled something onto a legal pad and passed it to her.

Deep breaths. We've got this.

The hearing proceeded with the standard formalities before Judge Abernathy addressed the matter at hand. "We're here regarding the motion for the compassionate release of inmate Darrell Boyd from Lieber Correctional Institution to Beaufort Memorial Hospital. Mr. Craig, please present your arguments."

Emmett rose, buttoning his suit jacket as he moved to the podium. "Thank you, Your Honor. Darrell Boyd has been diagnosed with stage four colon cancer that has metastasized to his liver. The prison medical facility is not equipped to provide the level of care he requires. Dr. Samuel Patel, an oncologist at Memorial, has reviewed Mr. Boyd's medical records and confirms the necessity of specialized treatment unavailable at Lieber."

He presented the court with Dr. Patel's affidavit and Darrell's medical records, which Judge Abernathy reviewed carefully before passing to the clerk.

"Mr. Boyd's condition is rapidly deteriorating," Emmett continued. "The prison doctor estimates he has four to six months to live. Transfer to Memorial would allow for palliative care that would ease his suffering during his remaining time."

"And who would cover the costs of this specialized care?" Judge Abernathy inquired.

Emmett glanced briefly at Tracey. "The Boyd family would cover any expenses beyond what the Department of Corrections would typically provide."

With the judge's permission, Solicitor Jennings approached the podium. "Your Honor, while the state acknowledges Mr. Boyd's medical condition, we oppose this *transfer* on several grounds. First, the security protocols at Beaufort Memorial are not equivalent to those at a maximum-security facility like Lieber. Mr. Boyd was convicted of second degree murder and sentenced to life without parole."

"Mr. Boyd can barely walk." Emmett interjected. "He poses no flight risk."

Jennings continued. "Nevertheless, precedent requires that security considerations remain paramount. Additionally, the state contends that adequate medical care can be provided within the correctional system, possibly through transfer to a medical prison facility rather than a civilian hospital."

Judge Abernathy removed his glasses, cleaning them thoughtfully. "Mr. Jennings, the medical reports indicate that the prison system's facilities cannot provide the specialized care Mr. Boyd requires."

"The reports are based on Dr. Patel's assessment, Your Honor. The state would request an independent evaluation before a civilian hospital transfer is approved."

Emmett sensed Tracey shifting beside him. He glanced at her, noting the turmoil on her face. Another evaluation meant more delays, and time was not on Darrell's side.

"Your Honor," Emmett argued, "any delay could be detrimental to Mr. Boyd's condition. Dr. Patel is a respected oncologist with no connection to the defense. His assessment should be sufficient."

Judge Abernathy considered this. "I'm inclined to agree, Mr. Jennings. Unless you have evidence that Dr. Patel's evaluation is flawed?"

Jennings hesitated. "No direct evidence, Your Honor. But the state would like to note for the record that this request could coincide with a renewed interest in the Boyd case by this new defense counsel."

"Objection." Emmett called out. "My being the new defense counsel is irrelevant to the medical transfer request. Mr. Boyd is terminally ill."

"Sustained," Judge Abernathy ruled. "Mr. Jennings, please limit your arguments to the matter at hand."

"Yes, Your Honor," he acknowledged. "The state also wishes to enter an objection from the victim's family." He gestured toward the Whitakers. "They oppose this transfer on both principle and practical grounds."

Judge Abernathy looked over his glasses which had slid down his nose. "While I respect the Whitaker family's position, their objection does not override the legal standards for prisoner medical care."

From the gallery, Alex stood. "Your Honor, if I may address the court?"

Judge Abernathy frowned. "Mr. Whitaker, this is not a victim impact hearing. Your written objection has been noted."

"My father was murdered by Darrell Boyd," Alex persisted. "Our family has concerns that—"

"Mr. Whitaker," Judge Abernathy interrupted, his voice stern. "Please be seated or I will have you removed from my courtroom."

After a tense moment, Alex sat down, his face reddened with barely contained anger.

Emmett did his best to keep the smirk he felt off his face. He thanked God that this hearing was going in the right direction and Abernathy hadn't been influenced by Alex's attempts.

Judge Abernathy turned back to the attorneys. "I've reviewed the medical evidence and find it compelling. However, I'm also mindful of security concerns. I will approve the medical transfer with the following conditions: Mr. Boyd will remain under guard at all times. The Department of Corrections will determine appropriate security measures. And the medical transfer is approved specifically for medical treatment."

He eyed Emmett. "Mr. Craig, any legal proceedings related to Mr. Boyd's case must be conducted separately."

Relief washed over Emmett. "Thank you, Your Honor."

"Additionally," the judge continued, "I'm ordering bi-weekly updates on Mr. Boyd's condition from the treating physician. The first such update will be due two weeks from the date of the transfer to Beaufort Memorial."

With that, Judge Abernathy closed the hearing, and the bailiff called the next case. As people began to move around the courtroom, Emmett turned to Tracey, whose eyes shone with unshed tears.

He sat down next to her. "Are you okay?"

She nodded. "I'm good. What's next?"

"I'll have to coordinate with the Department of Corrections, but hopefully by the end of the week he can be transferred to Beaufort Memorial." Emmett gathered his papers, conscious of the Whitakers watching them from across the room. "Let's get out of here."

They had nearly reached the door when Alex intercepted them. "After what Darrell did to my father, he deserves to suffer."

The way Tracey narrowed her eyes, Emmett had a feeling she was close to exploding.

"Alex." Rachel placed a restraining hand on her brother's arm. "That's enough. This isn't the place." She turned to Tracey, her expression less hostile than Alex's. "Tracey, it's been a long time. I'm sorry about your father's illness."

Emmett glanced at Tracey who appeared startled. He was leery of Rachel's stance as well. While she wasn't brash like her brother, he recalled Rachel being one of those mean girls in school.

Tracey looked at him before responding. "Thank you, Rachel."

Rachel nodded. "Life has changed so much since.. . well, since everything happened." She tucked a strand of blonde hair behind her ear. "Mother asks about you sometimes. She thinks about you and your mother often."

Alex scoffed, but Rachel shot him a warning look.

"How is Helen?" Tracey asked.

"She has her good days and bad days," Rachel said with a sigh. "Losing Dad broke something in her that never quite healed. I think she'd like to see you sometime, under better circumstances than this."

"Rachel," Alex's voice held a note of warning. "We need to go check on Mother. You know she will be worried."

Rachel nodded, giving Tracey one last look. "Take care of yourself, Tracey."

Emmett wasn't surprised that Helen Whitaker wasn't here. He'd heard she'd become a bit of a recluse. But her children certainly made sure they'd thrown around their weight.

He guided Tracey out of the courtroom, not stopping until they reached the relative privacy of the courthouse steps. There, Tracey drew a shuddering breath, her composure finally cracking. "He's dying. And he's been doing his time. There was no need for Alex to be this cruel, saying all that in the courtroom."

Her pain was palpable, and Emmett found himself wanting to shield her from it. "Today we won a small victory. Let's focus on that."

Tracey swiped at her eyes, regaining her composure with visible effort. "You're right. All that matters is getting my father the care he needs. When can I see him?"

"I can drive you to Lieber tomorrow if you would like. Once the medical transfer is processed, they'll begin arrangements to move him."

They descended the courthouse steps, and Emmett noticed several reporters approaching with notepads in hand. He wanted to kick himself for not leading Tracey out another door.

"Ms. Boyd! How does it feel to be back in Beaufort? Will you be staying long?"

"No comment." Emmett intervened. With a protective arm around her shoulders, he guided her toward the parking lot.

"Mr. Craig! Are you reopening the Boyd case? Is new evidence being examined?"

He hated that these vultures were here today. It probably didn't help that folks thought he was taking on another murder case. He'd provided the perfect recipe for the media hounds looking for another story. But this case was nothing like the Langley case.

Emmett ignored the questions, focusing instead on getting Tracey safely to her car. Thankfully, no one followed them. Tracey fumbled with her key fob. Once she swung the door open, she climbed inside and slumped against the seat. A thin sheen of perspiration showed on her forehead and upper lip. "I don't need those people around Sweetgrass or my son."

The mention of her son reminded Emmett of the further complications she faced. "Do you have other family in Beaufort besides your aunt? I mean just in case any reporters show up at the Sweetgrass."

He already knew the answer to his question, but he wanted to hear from Tracey.

She didn't look at him and placed her hands in her lap. "On my dad's side, it's just Aunt Edna. My mother's family lives up north. Jayden's father was Jordan Harris. You might remember him. He played varsity basketball."

Emmett nodded. "I remember him being a star player even as a sophomore."

"He died when Jayden was almost three. Car accident." Her voice caught slightly. "His family and I... we've had our differences. They tried to get custody of Jayden after my father was convicted."

Emmett face grew heated. "What? Why? They weren't trying to use your father's conviction against you."

"That's exactly what Lydia Harris intended to do. They argued I was emotionally unstable, unfit to parent just because I wouldn't let them see Jayden. I knew how they felt about my dad being charged. I just didn't want my son around them." She bit her lip. "It was the last straw for me. Losing Jordan. And then everything with my father. When the judge ruled in my favor, I left. Made a clean break from this place."

"And now you're back."

She closed her eyes briefly. "It's like I never left."

She spoke so low he almost didn't hear her. He felt responsible for putting her through this. "For what it's worth, I think you're handling it all remarkably well."

Her eyes popped open, and a ghost of a smile touched her lips. "You wouldn't say that if you could see inside my head, Redd."

He chuckled, pleased to see her comfort with him. "I suppose not. But sometimes just showing up and facing it all counts as courage."

Tracey straightened in her seat. "I need to get back to Jayden. Tomorrow, then? To see my father?"

Emmett stepped away. "I'll be happy to drive. How about eight o'clock? It's about a two-hour drive to Lieber, so we should arrive by ten."

She nodded. "Thank you in advance for the ride. And for everything today. I don't think I could have faced that alone."

"I will make sure that you don't face anything alone, Tracey." The words slipped out easily, but Emmett meant them.

Tracey held his gaze for a moment longer. Something unspoken passed between them. She closed her car door and cranked the car's engine.

Watching her go, Emmett felt that despite all his preparation for this case, he hadn't been prepared for Tracey Boyd. The long ago teenage crush rushed back, turning into something he hadn't been expecting. But his thoughts were completely off-limits.

He had a job to do.

Emmett headed to his own car. After he climbed in, the hairs on the back of his neck stood up. He turned on the engine and locked himself inside the car. That familiar eerie sensation of being watched crept over him. He glanced in his rearview mirror, scanning the parking lot for the pickup truck he'd seen lurking near his house. Nothing obvious caught his eye, but the feeling persisted.

He looked down at his hands. The scrapes on his palms from the night at The Blue Heron were healing, the raw skin now pink and tender rather than angry red. The reminder of the other night caused him a brief bit of panic. If his presence in this case was attracting the media, what else would it bring?

After his talk with Tracey, the last thing he wanted to do was bring *his* trouble to Boyd's family. He wasn't even sure what he was dealing with. Before he pulled off, he checked his mirrors once more, continuing to be alert as he drove away.

Chapter 13

Sweetgrass Bed & Breakfast
Monday, May 19 at 2:35 p.m. EST

The courthouse hearing had consumed all her mental energy, but Tracey returned to the Sweetgrass restless with unease. She half-expected reporters to show up at the bed-and-breakfast, scaring off the nice couple who'd checked in last night. Empty-nesters down from New Jersey, this was the Robertsons' first getaway vacation together in decades. She'd enjoyed talking to them last night and loved seeing her aunt in action, making her guests feel at home.

The Robertsons were out shopping, and Jayden, who didn't normally take afternoon naps, was knocked out. Her little boy had been like the Energizer bunny since they arrived on Saturday. Finally tuckered out after a hearty lunch, Tracey was grateful for the quiet since Jayden woke this morning with questions she didn't know how to answer. Why did she need to go see a judge? Why couldn't they just help Granddad since he was sick? All good questions.

She barely understood what went down this morning herself. Sitting in the family room, she scrolled through her inbox and winced at the number of unread messages. Maybe this wasn't a good idea. She'd barely been gone one day. A message from Mia caught her eye.

Subject: Project Delayed!

Tracey clicked the email, bracing herself for what she was about to read.

Tracey, hope you're doing okay with family stuff. Guess what? There will be some construction delays in the east wing. Regina changed the design again this morning as if that wasn't going to cause a delay. She upset the foreman so much he threatened to pull out of the agreement.

Don't worry about any of this. Henry was able to smooth things over as usual. I just wanted to give you a heads up just in case your boss reaches out. Focus on what you need to do there.

LMK if you need anything!

Mia.

Below that was a message from Javier.

Subject: Brochure Design Revisions #8

Tracey, I really hope you're NOT reading this email. But knowing you and how you stay on top of things, attached are the latest mockups for the brochure. If you have two minutes to look and give feedback, that would be awesome.

Just know by the time you see these revisions, Regina might change her mind again... because of course, she will.

Take care!

Javier

Part of her was relieved to be away from the daily drama at the Morrison, but guilt nagged at her for leaving her colleagues to deal with Regina. Tracey decided it was best to close her laptop.

"Bad news from work?" Edna asked, entering with a basket of fresh linens.

"The usual. My boss making impossible demands and blaming everyone else when things go wrong."

Edna shook her head. "I'm glad you're getting a bit of a break from that place." She set down the basket. "How are you holding up after this morning?"

Tracey's thoughts drifted back to the hearing, to the cold stares from the Whitaker siblings. "I don't understand. What harm would it do to let Dad spend his final months in a hospital instead of a prison cell?"

"Some people hold on to hate because it's easier than facing their own pain," Edna folded towels as she chatted. "Alex has always been a bully, even as a boy. He took after his daddy more than Helen would like to admit."

"James was like that too? I only remember him being nice to me growing up."

Edna twisted her mouth. "James could be charming when he wanted something. But he had a mean streak. Your daddy saw the good in him, always made excuses for his behavior."

"Why did Dad stay friends with him for so long if James was so difficult?"

"Loyalty. Your father valued it above almost everything else." Folding a pillowcase with practiced precision, she added. "Those two were thick as thieves since grade school. When your mama got sick, James and Helen were there every step of the way."

Tracey remembered something from the courthouse. "Helen wasn't at the courthouse."

Edna paused, folding a towel. "I imagine she wouldn't be. She doesn't seem to be around much anymore. I can't remember the last time I saw her."

"Were they really friends? Mom and Helen?"

"Oh, yes, very close once upon a time. Helen was devastated when your mama passed." Edna's hands stilled. "Something changed in her after that, though. She became more... withdrawn. And then when your daddy and James had their troubles. And then James was murdered."

"Sounds like she kind of died with him."

Edna resumed her folding. "Baby girl, grief can reshape a person. You probably aren't the same person you were five years ago."

Tracey considered this. "I guess so. I'm stronger than I was. Seeing Lydia and Diane yesterday would have taken me down. And then this morning, seeing Alex and Rachel."

Edna said quietly. "You're a survivor. Your mama would be proud. And your daddy is proud of you too."

Tracey bit her lip, but it didn't stop the tear that fell. "Do you need any help this afternoon? I'm guessing you have someone checking into the yellow room."

Edna smiled. "Yes, I'd welcome the extra hands." Her aunt dropped the towel she'd been folding. With lightning speed, the older woman moved toward Tracey and wrapped her arms around her.

"Chile, I have missed you being around here."

Tracey hugged her aunt back, realizing she also really missed this. Being home and around family who loved her.

Monday, May 19 at 4:04 p.m. EST

Tracey was dusting the antique dresser in the yellow room when Jayden's excited voice floated up from downstairs. Curious, Tracey moved to the window that overlooked the front yard. A sleek red Mazda was parked in the driveway. She frowned, wondering if the guest, a Miss Gladys Smithey, had arrived early. From Aunt Edna's description of the repeat patron, it didn't sound like she would've been driving such a sporty car.

Tracey headed downstairs. Hearing a familiar laugh coming from the sitting room, she smiled.

"Jay-Jay, you're like a mini-tornado," a woman's voice said. "How do you keep all that energy?"

"I eat my vegetables," Jayden raised his hands as if he was about to fly. "Mom says they give me superpowers."

Tracey laughed to herself as she stepped into the doorway. Her heart was already full from the hug she'd shared with her aunt earlier. Now the sight of her best friend perched on the edge of the sofa made her heart soar.

Charlene McMillan looked up, her face breaking into a wide smile. "Well, it's about time! I was beginning to think you were hiding from me." She rose to her feet, arms outstretched.

Tracey crossed the room in three quick strides and squeezed Charlene in a tight embrace.

Tracey stepped back to look at her friend properly. "Girl, look at you with these red braids."

Charlene moved her head back and forth, shaking the braids. "You know I have to change it up every so often. Speaking of red, Redd mentioned you might be coming back. I told him I was surprised. Last year when I visited, you didn't seem too enthused about coming back here."

It was true. No one was more surprised than Tracey. She appreciated that Charlene had maintained their friendship, despite the distance. Her friend had been the only person from home who visited Tracey in Florida. Aunt Edna wanted to come but could never get away.

"Jayden, why don't you go see if Aunt Edna needs help in the kitchen?" Tracey suggested. "I hear she is baking another one of those sweet potato pies."

"Yes! The best dessert ever!" Tracey and Charlene laughed as Jayden raced to the back of the bed-and-breakfast.

Charlene flopped onto the bench in front of the horseshoe window and patted a spot beside her. "You remember when we used to hang out here when we were younger? It felt like we could see so much from these windows.

Tracey sank down next to her friend. She'd been so busy upstairs she hadn't realized she was tired. "That brings back some nice memories."

Charlene studied her. "Girl, how are you holding up? I know this hasn't been easy for you."

"Honestly? I don't know. We had the hearing this morning for getting my dad transferred. Alex and Rachel showed up."

Charlene sucked in a breath. "No, they didn't?"

"The Whitakers had the solicitor practically accuse us of trying to help my father escape. Escape to what? He's dying, Charlene."

Charlene placed her hand on Tracey's arm. "I'm sorry."

Tracey clutched her friend's hand in hers. "No, I'm sorry. You all lost Mr. Mac. How is your family holding up?"

Charlene grimaced. "We're moving forward as much as we can. I can tell Mama is really lonely and missing him. I've been back here about a month myself."

"Wow, it's incredible how we all end up coming back home." Tracey frowned. "Do you know how long Emmett, I mean Redd, has been back?"

Charlene grinned. "Checking up on him, are you?"

Tracey laughed. "He's been really helpful. I don't know how I would have gotten through this morning without him. It's just that, I did read about his previous case."

"Oh, that." Charlene sighed. "Redd has been back for about two years now. Speaking of death, his father passed away. I think he originally came back to take care of his father's funeral, but ended up staying. He mentioned to Kenny that he was tired of Atlanta. Anyhow, he decided to start his own law practice. He might have bit off more than he bargained for with the Langley case."

"They say Emmett got him off on a technicality, but a lot of people thought Langley did it. I just wondered if any of that would blow back on my dad."

Charlene reached over to squeeze her hand. "Redd is really good at what he does. My dad left his caseload to him and you know my dad was particular about who he trusted and recommended. I believe your dad is in good hands. Besides, Redd needs a break. He really was doing what he could to help his client."

Tracey nodded. "I believe that about him. He's going to drive me to see my dad tomorrow."

A mischievous glint appeared in Charlene's eyes. "Really? You two are spending a lot of time together."

Tracey rolled her eyes. "It's strictly professional."

"Mmhmm. You know Redd had the biggest crush on you back in the day, right?"

Tracey laughed in disbelief. "What? No, he didn't."

"Girl, please. Every time you came over to my house, that boy found some excuse to hang around. Always asking if you were coming to the house. Kenny used to tease him something awful about it."

Tracey tilted her head, recalling how she would catch him staring at her. She would do the same. But she was curious about him. Redd was so different from everyone else. He was shy around her at the Mac's house, but they would talk to each other, especially in the library. He seemed to open up when they were alone, almost like he were a different person.

Charlene went on, "My parents practically adopted Redd. They didn't seem to mind him being over at our house. I don't know if you remember, but his family was a bit of a mess."

A pang of sympathy went through Tracey. She remembered hearing vague stories about Emmett's troubled home life, though she'd never known the details. "Well, I had a chance to watch him in action in the courtroom, he's very confident. He knows his stuff."

"Law school will do that to you," Charlene agreed. "Well, I better get to the house before Mama starts looking for me. When you're back in your parent's house, it's like you never left and made it on your own."

"I will stop by and see your mom before we head back. Thanks for coming by," Tracey said, walking her friend to the door. "It means a lot."

Charlene pulled her into another hug. "I'm here whenever you need me, Tracey. Day or night. And hey—"she lowered her voice, "—don't be too hard on yourself tomorrow, okay? Whatever happens with your dad, you're doing the right thing just by showing up."

"Thank you."

"Oh, and remember, Redd is good people. I think you two have a lot more in common than you both know. Plus, you're in good hands with him."

After Charlene left, Tracey retreated to her room, closing the door behind her. She knew Jayden would be fine with Aunt Edna.

She needed to do something that she'd put off for too long. The unopened letter from her father was in her suitcase. She wasn't really sure why she still hadn't opened it. Tracey picked it up, turning the envelope over in her hands. With trembling fingers, she gently pulled out the single sheet of paper and unfolded it.

Tracey,

I know it's been a long time. I've respected your wishes by not trying to contact you, though it's been the hardest thing I've ever done. Edna tells me you're doing well in Florida, and that Jayden is growing into a fine boy. I'm glad for that.

I'm writing now because time isn't on my side anymore. The doctors say I have cancer, and it's spread too far for treatment to do much good. I don't tell you this for sympathy, but because there are things that need to be said before I'm gone.

I think what hurts me more than anything is you thinking I'm a murderer. I didn't kill James. I know you heard the evidence at the trial, saw the anger between us that last day. I can't blame you for doubting me. But I swear on your mother's memory, I am innocent.

If you can find it in your heart to visit, I would be grateful for the chance to explain things I couldn't tell you before. If not, I understand. Either way, please know that I have loved you every day of your life, and my greatest regret is the pain my situation has caused you and Jayden.

All my love, Dad

Tracey read the letter twice more, tears blurring the words. The handwriting was shakier than she remembered, evidence of her father's declining health.

And he'd never invoke her mother's memory lightly.

Setting the letter aside, Tracey moved to the window and gazed out at the garden below. Tomorrow she would face her father and look into his eyes. Should she even be concerned if he had committed the violence he'd been convicted of? No.

She'd lost her mother to cancer twenty years ago, right before Tracey reached puberty. The hardest thing at that time in her life was saying goodbye to her mother. It seemed unfair to have to lose her only living parent to another form of cancer.

Chapter 14

Sweetgrass Bed & Breakfast
Tuesday, May 20 at 7:55 a.m. EST

Emmett arrived at Sweetgrass five minutes earlier than their agreed meeting time. He sat in his car for a moment, gathering his thoughts. The prison visit ahead would be emotionally charged for Tracey, and also for him as well. Last night he couldn't help but thinking about how Tracey's reunion with her estranged father would remind him of his missed opportunity.

He'd returned to bury his father. Richard seemed to be fine with having a life separate from his children.

Emmett sighed and stepped out of the car, straightening his tie. He'd opted for a suit, wanting to provide Tracey with as much professional support as possible. Lieber Correctional wasn't an easy place to visit.

Edna opened the door before he could knock, greeting him with a knowing smile that reminded him uncomfortably of his conversation with Tracey's aunt the previous week.

"Look at you! Right on time," she said, stepping aside to let him enter. "Tracey's just finishing up. Can I get you some coffee?"

"No, thank you, Miss Boyd. We should probably get on the road."

Edna nodded, studying him. "Jayden's still asleep. The boy was up half the night with questions about his grandfather. Tracey had a hard time settling him down."

Emmett could imagine how difficult those conversations must have been. "Is Jayden disappointed about not going today?"

"He understands it's just for his mama this first time." Edna lowered her voice. "Between you and me, I think Tracey needs alone time with her father. Too much has been left unsaid between them."

Tracey appeared at the top of the stairs. She wore dark gray pants with a white shirt. What appeared to be a light pink sweater was draped over her arm. Despite her composed appearance, the tension in her shoulders and the weariness around her eyes told Emmett she'd had a restless night.

She headed down the stairs, her shoes softly clopping on the mahogany staircase. Her eyes met his briefly. "Good morning."

He caught himself staring a bit too long. "Morning."

"Call me when you're heading back," Edna instructed, pulling Tracey into a fierce hug. "And tell that hardheaded brother of mine I'll be up to see him once he's settled at Beaufort Memorial."

They walked toward his car without exchanging any more words. Emmett opened the passenger door for her before climbing in himself. The first thirty minutes of the drive passed in silence, but he wasn't bothered by the quiet. He sensed Tracey needed this time to prepare herself.

It wasn't until they were on the highway that Tracey spoke. "I read his letter." Her eyes fixed on the landscape passing outside her window. "He'd sent me a letter a few weeks ago, but I just opened it last night. Isn't that crazy?"

Emmett glanced at her. "Nothing wrong with waiting until you're ready. What did he say?"

"That he's innocent." She turned to look at him directly. "He swore on my mother's memory that he didn't kill James Whitaker."

"Do you believe him?"

Tracey admitted after a long pause. "I want to. But I saw him that day, Emmett. The day before James was killed. I've never seen my father so angry. He and James were shouting, pushing each other. I thought they were going to throw punches. It was that bad."

"People can be angry without being killers." He pointed out. "And the evidence against your father seemed too convenient. Plus, your father had no history of violence. No witnesses placed him at the scene during the estimated time of death. And the coroner's report indicated James could have been killed by anyone. Mr. Mac tried to hone in on the fact that it could have been someone shorter or with less strength than your father."

Tracey turned to him. "I remember when Mr. Mac cross-examined the coroner."

Emmett nodded. "He tried hard to establish reasonable doubt. From his notes, he spent months investigating alternative suspects, trying to find the real killer."

"Did he get anywhere with that?"

"He looked into Thad Jenkins. That's the employee James fired who made threats against the company. But Jenkins had an ironclad alibi for the night of the murder. He was at his sister's wedding."

Tracey frowned. "What about the Whitaker family? Did Mr. Mac ever look into them?"

Emmett's mind went back to Mr. Mac's note. He wasn't really sure how much to say to Tracey. "I'm going through all of Mr. Mac's notes, following up on leads he might have missed. Mrs. Mac told me something interesting when I saw her last week."

"What's that?"

"She said in the months before he died, Mr. Mac became consumed with your father's case. Staying up late to work on it. She believed he was onto something significant."

Emmett hesitated. "Miss Violet thinks the stress of whatever he discovered might have contributed to his heart attack."

Tracey's eyes widened. "You're saying Mr. Mac might have found something that got him killed?"

"No, no." Emmett said quickly. "But I do think he was closing in on something that could've helped your father. I just need to figure out what it was."

"Why are you so convinced he's innocent?" Tracey asked, studying him intently.

Emmett felt his face grow hot under her stare. "Mr. Mac believed in your father's innocence. That carries weight with me. And...I've seen what happens when the justice system gets it wrong. From both sides."

Tracey asked. "You mean the Preston Langley case?"

Emmett's eyes widened slightly behind his glasses.

"Remember, I found you on Google. Technical grounds, despite substantial evidence," she quoted from the article she'd read. "The victim's family was really upset."

That was an understatement. "Because of attorney-client privilege, I can neither confirm nor deny your insinuation without being disbarred. But let's just say I've learned some hard lessons."

Her focus remained intently on him. "And yet here you are, taking on another murder case. Is this what you did in Atlanta too?"

It took him a minute to answer.

She really had been looking into him.

He wasn't sure if he was flattered or scared. "Yes, I've always been a defense attorney. But I hadn't taken on criminal cases like this until coming back here."

He hoped she didn't ask any more about it. Emmett was treading a thin line, and they should be focused on what he could for her father. There was nothing Emmett could do to fix his past mistake.

Thankfully, Tracey asked, "What should I expect today? At the prison?"

Grateful for the subject change, Emmett outlined the security procedures and reminded her about the limitations on physical contact.

Tracey sounded small. "I haven't seen him since I moved to Florida. That's five years! That must seem awful to you?"

Emmett assured her. "I'm not one to judge, Tracey. My father and I didn't have the best relationship before he died. Your father and you are blessed to have this time together."

For the rest of the drive, they talked about other topics. Tracey mentioned her marketing job at the Morrison, while Emmett shared his adventures of renovating the old house.

"I love old houses. I remember helping Mama and Aunt Edna decorate the Sweetgrass when they first opened it. I was still young, but it was fun painting and watching how the rooms came together."

He wondered about the bed-and-breakfast. "Who owned the house?"

"The house has been in my dad's family for years. When my grandmother died, Aunt Edna and my dad weren't sure what to do with it being so big. Mama suggested they turn it into a bed-and-breakfast."

He raised an eyebrow. "I didn't know that. Maybe you can give me some tips on my house. It's where I grew up, but I'm making it my own."

Tracey looked at him. "I would love to see what you're doing to the place."

He glanced at her, surprised by her gesture. For a moment, he wondered if Tracey had forgotten where they were headed, just as he had. The conversation had shifted from painful pasts to something lighter, more normal. It could have been their way of spending time in the car or avoiding talking about the pending visit. Either way, the conversation was pleasant. Quite comfortable.

Emmett grinned. "Well, I'm warning you, it's a work in progress. Kenny is going to help me knock down the wall between the kitchen and the living room."

"Open concept! Now that's a major task," Tracey replied. "I actually painted those blue rocking chairs on the porch at Sweetgrass my last summer before moving to Florida. It's been good helping Aunt Edna the past few days."

He glanced at her, happy to hear she had good memories and some good moments since she'd been back.

As they approached Lieber Correctional, Emmett's pulse quickened. He knew exactly the moment when Tracey's nerves ramped up. If only it weren't unprofessional to reach over and touch her hands that she was now wringing together in her lap.

Chapter 15

Lieberman Correctional Institution
Tuesday, May 20 at 9:57 a.m. EST

The sprawling complex of concrete and steel surrounded by multiple layers of barbed wire fencing came into view. Emmett felt Tracey tense beside him as they approached the main gate. This early on a Tuesday, the parking lot was nearly empty. Emmett found a spot close to the entrance and turned off the engine. Before Tracey could open her door, he placed a gentle hand on her arm.

"Take a moment," he advised. "There's no rush."

She nodded, drawing a deep breath and releasing it slowly. "I keep thinking about what I'm going to say to him. Five years of silence, and now he's dying... Where do we even begin?"

"Sometimes it's enough just to be present," Emmett said. "Words aren't always necessary."

Tracey gave him a grateful look. "Thank you for coming with me. I don't think I could have done this alone."

"You're stronger than you give yourself credit for," Emmett replied. "But I'm glad to be here."

IDs checked, forms signed, belongings surrendered to lockers. Tracey submitted to the security screening with quiet dignity, though Emmett noticed her hands trembling slightly as she removed her cardigan and shoes for inspection.

A guard led them down a series of corridors, each separated by heavy metal doors that closed with a definitive clang behind them. A combination of industrial cleaner, sweat, and stale air grew stronger as they approached the visitation area.

"Your father's in the medical wing," the guard explained as they walked. "Special arrangements have been made for a private visit, given the circumstances."

Emmett glanced at Tracey, who walked beside him. She was back to wringing her hands.

The room they were led to was small. There was hardly room for a table and three chairs. Unlike the regular visitation area, with its noisy chaos and watchful guards, this space offered a semblance of privacy. A concession to a dying man and his estranged daughter.

"Boyd will be brought in shortly," the guard informed them before stepping outside the door.

Tracey stood near the table, looking lost. Emmett moved to her side. "Do you want me to stay for the beginning, or would you prefer some time alone with him first?"

She hesitated. "Maybe... maybe just the first few minutes?"

"Of course," he agreed. He was happy to be a buffer for what could be an awkward reunion.

The door opened, and two guards appeared escorting Darrell Boyd. Emmett heard Tracey's sharp intake of breath and instinctively moved closer to her side.

Darrell shuffled into the room, arms and ankles shackled. His prison jumpsuit hung loosely on his gaunt frame. His shoulders stooped with the effort of walking. But then his eyes landed on Tracey.

"Tracey?" he said, his voice hoarse. "Is it really you?"

"Hi, Daddy."

The guards helped Darrell to a chair before stepping back. "We'll be right outside," one of them said. "You have one hour."

An awkward silence fell as the guards exited. Darrell stared at his daughter as if trying to memorize her face. Tracey seemed unable to look directly at him, her gaze darting around the room.

Emmett cleared his throat gently. "Mr. Boyd, we've filed the medical transfer paperwork. You should be moved to Beaufort Memorial by the end of the week."

Darrell nodded, but his eyes never left Tracey. "Thank you, Mr. Craig." He paused. "You look good, baby girl. Florida must agree with you."

"It's different," Tracey managed. "Kind of similar to Beaufort, but not."

"Jayden," Darrell's voice cracked. "How's my grandson?"

"He's good. Growing so fast. Smart. He..." Tracey faltered. "He can't wait to see you."

"I'd like that," Darrell said. "More than anything."

Emmett sensed it was time for him to step back, to give them the space they needed. He rose from his chair. "We don't have much time, so I'll be right outside if you need me."

Tracey shot him a look, her eyes wide.

Darrell murmured his thanks as Emmett moved toward the door.

As he exited, Emmett heard Darrell's voice, thick with emotion. "I didn't think you'd come."

When the door closed behind him, Emmett's thoughts drifted to his own father. Watching Tracey reunite with her father reminded Emmett of his missed opportunity with his own father.

Tuesday, May 20 at 10:16 a.m. EST

After Emmett left, silence filled the small room. Tracey found herself unable to look directly at her father, instead focusing on her tightly clasped hands in her lap. The man across from her bore little resemblance to the strong, confident father she remembered.

"Tracey, look at me. I know it's hard."

She lifted her eyes. Before she could stop it, a tear slid down her cheek. "I'm sorry I stayed away so long. I wanted to believe you. In the beginning, I did. But the evidence, the jury..."

"I know, baby girl." He laid his hand across the table, the bones prominent beneath paper-thin skin. "You did what you had to do. Taking Jayden away and making a new life. That is what you needed to do."

"But I left you alone. Here," she whispered, guilt washing over her.

"You protected your son," Darrell stated firmly. "Just like I tried to protect you. But I failed. I've been nothing but proud of you, Tracey. Never blamed you for leaving. Never stopped loving you."

"I'm so sorry." She held her hands over her face.

"Shhh," Darrell soothed. "You're here now. That's what matters."

When her tears subsided, Tracey looked at her father with new clarity. "We need to fix this. Find who really killed James."

"Mr. Mac wouldn't give up. He kept digging for answers. Until his heart gave out on him."

Tracey asked, leaning forward. "It's been seven years. What could he have found before he died that made him want to leave your case to Redd?"

Darrell raised his eyebrow. "Red?"

Tracey blushed. "Your lawyer. I don't know if you remember the redhead boy who hung around Kenny."

Her father's eyes widened. "What? I knew that young man looked familiar. I didn't know why Mac trusted him, other than he seems like a good man. I believe he'll keep fighting even after I'm gone."

She wasn't ready to think about her dad being gone. They'd just reunited after all this time. "Did Mr. Mac have questions the last time he saw you?"

Darrell frowned, "Yes, he did. Mac wanted to know more about *that* company. I think they were named Coastal Developments. I don't even know where they came from, but they proposed this massive resort project. James was all excited about it. Then things turned strange. When I pushed for details, James just shut me out."

"Seems like he should have been smarter."

"I agree." Her father's eyes flashed with anger, but then he deflated from the effort. "James had brought Alex more into the company. He wouldn't admit it, but he gave that boy too much freedom. Alex didn't have the experience. I walked in on them shouting at each other once. James slammed his fist on the desk and said something like,

'You've gone too far this time.' When they saw me, they both clammed up."

Tracey thought about how Alex had showed up at the courthouse with his sister. Why were they really so bent on keeping her father from having medical care?

When the guard knocked on the door to signal their time was ending, Tracey stood, reluctant to leave.

"I'll bring Jayden to see you once you're settled at the hospital."

Darrell nodded, his eyes bright with unshed tears. "Tell him his grandpa can't wait to see him."

Tracey moved around the table and, ignoring prison protocol, embraced her father gently. She could feel every bone in his back through the thin fabric of his jumpsuit, a stark reminder of the cancer eating away at him.

"I love you, Daddy," she whispered.

"I love you too, baby girl," he replied, his voice rough with emotion. "Always have. Always will."

When Tracey stepped into the corridor, she found Emmett waiting on a nearby chair. She knew her eyes were probably red-rimmed, but she didn't care.

"Everything okay?" Emmett asked, rising to meet her.

"You got to help him, Redd. We have to find out who got away with murder."

Chapter 16

Beaufort, South Carolina
Tuesday, May 20 at 7:49 p.m. EST

Emmett laid on his couch after the drive, more exhausted than he realized. Between his obsessive nature with this case and a lot of sleepless nights, he was beyond sleep-deprived. His intentions were to catch an afternoon nap. He'd hung up his suit coat and pulled off his socks and shoes. Before drifting off to sleep on his couch, he'd ripped off his tie and unbuttoned his shirt. After an hour, he found himself wide awake thinking about Tracey's plea.

We have to find out who got away with murder.

We? No, Tracey, not we. I do.

It was his job. Almost his purpose these days. With this case, his instincts were firing on all cylinders again. Something wasn't right and based on what he'd gathered from Jack's investigation, he needed to go back to the beginning.

Who had motive and what set someone off so much they'd bashed James Whitaker in the head? Someone either snuck up on James while he was in his office or the man had turned his back on a visitor, not knowing how much rage his attacker was about to literally hurl at him.

The person who killed James also had access to the office safe. It seemed logical that the person witnessed the intense argument between James and Darrell the previous day. Why else would the real murderer deposit the murder weapon and the money in Darrell's truck? From his conversation with Edna last week, Darrell always parked his truck in the shed behind the Sweetgrass. The person could have easily planted the evidence under the cover of darkness.

Emmett stood and stretched, feeling his muscles and joints ache from the uncomfortable couch and consistent lack of exercise. He moved to the window, watching the fading daylight cast long shadows across his lawn. He had a sinking feeling there were some twists to this case that would surprise him.

If only he could figure out how Langley was involved. He didn't want to face the man again, but he might have to soon. Langley was a shrewd business owner who had to have some reason for wanting to deal with Whitaker.

Emmett also needed to figure out what was going on internally between father and son. James trusted his son enough to bring him into the business. Had Alex messed up somewhere?

Alex knows something.

That's what Mr. Mac wrote on that note he'd tucked away in his Bible.

Certainly if someone murdered Emmett's dad, no matter how rocky their relationship, he would have been angry, wanting the murderer to pay. But something about Alex's behavior struck Emmett as off. Like why show up at Mr. Mac's funeral? And Darrell was dying. It was macabre to want the man to suffer.

No matter how harsh his own father had treated him growing up, Emmett hated his dad was too prideful to reach out. Richard Craig had suffered alone before he left this world. Cirrhosis of the liver, along with several other health issues, had taken him from this world. None of his children, including Emmett, had reconciled with their father.

That acute pain hit hard watching Tracey react to her father and vice versa. Somehow, he didn't want father and daughter to have their last moments filled with this wrongful conviction hanging over their heads. Darrell fighting to stay alive for a few more months would be difficult enough.

Emmett grabbed his phone off the coffee table and dialed.

"Daniels," came the gruff answer after two rings.

"It's Emmett. I need your help with something."

Jack chuckled. "I figured you would call eventually. What's on your mind?"

"I really want to talk to the Whitakers."

Jack let out a long sigh on the other end. "That will not be easy. We never had a conversation with Helen. She had a breakdown and her son wouldn't let us near her."

"Did you talk to Alex or his sister Rachel?"

"I believe Mac talked to the sister. To be honest, she wasn't much help. She wasn't involved in the business and really didn't get along with the dad. She was upset about his murder, but she had nothing to offer. Alex fussed out Mac for trying. He'd determined it was Darrell and stuck to his opinion. Didn't you say you ran into him?"

"I have. More times than I care for. I'm wondering why Mr. Mac wrote his name down." Emmett could see the scribbled note in his mind.

Alex knows something.

What did he know? Did Mr. Mac think Alex knew the real killer? If so, why pin the murder on Darrell? Then another thought hit him.

What if Alex was the killer?

Jack cleared his throat, interrupting Emmett's thoughts. "If Mac had time to dig a little deeper into the company's finances, he might have been able to subpoena Alex. Got him on the stand. Right now? I just don't know."

Emmett would worry about Alex later. It might be to their benefit that the man didn't know they suspected him of anything. He switched gears. "Okay, what about the fired employee? Thad Jenkins?"

"The guy who threatened Whitaker?" Jack's tone grew serious. "Mac looked into him years ago. Guy had an ironclad alibi for the night of the murder. I can pull up the file, but I believe security footage showed him at his sister's wedding in Greenville. That's a three and half hour drive."

"I want to come at him differently. He might know something about what was happening at the company before the murder. According to the trial transcripts, he was fired a week before James was killed. I want to know why and what the atmosphere around the company was like."

"That's an interesting angle. Let me guess. You want to see if Mr. Jenkins noticed anything or may have been fired for some crazy reason?"

"Well, isn't that what he claimed? That he was fired without cause. I think for me to get my foot into how to reopen this case, I need to know what was happening back then."

"Well, last I heard, he's working at Crawford Construction on the new office complex project. I can see if we could catch him there tomorrow."

Emmett checked his calendar. "That sounds good. Maybe we can head out during their lunch break."

"Sounds like a plan." Jack's voice lowered. "Did you see Darrell today? How's he doing? Mac was telling me before he died how much he wanted to see his daughter."

"Yes, I drove her to Leiber. It was a pretty emotional day."

"I bet. I know the Boyd sister. Edna used to keep in touch with Mac and sometimes harass me for information. How is the daughter feeling about everything?"

"That's why I called. She wants to find out who framed her dad."

Tracey and Edna deserved the truth. But first, Emmett needed to understand exactly what they were dealing with. Who were all the players with motive to want James Whitaker dead? According to his mentor, the family had motive and should have been investigated more thoroughly.

Highway 21 Construction Site
Wednesday, May 21 at 11:52 a.m. EST

The mid-afternoon sun sat high in the sky over the construction site where a new office complex was taking shape. Heavy machinery, including a large crane carrying steel bars, captured Emmett's attention after he parked his car beside Jack's weathered Ford pickup. His BMW appeared out of place among the workers' trucks and equipment. At least he'd dressed down a bit, opting for a polo shirt and dark jeans. He hoped he didn't look like a lawyer.

Jack greeted him, and they began walking outside the metal fence that surrounded the site. The older man sported gray stubble on his face this morning. "I found Jenkins's phone number and called him. He wasn't too excited about this visit, but he'd heard about Darrell's illness and will hear us out." Jack nodded toward the man. "That's him. Still built like a linebacker."

Thad Jenkins was broad-shouldered and solid, despite being in his mid-fifties. He wore a hard hat, and even from a distance, Emmett could see the focused intensity in his movements.

"Are you sure he doesn't mind talking to us?" Emmett asked as the man approached.

Jack glanced at him. "It was some ugly business back then. If Jenkins didn't have his alibi, he could have easily been targeted for James's murder."

They waited until Jenkins stood in front of them. His eyes narrowed as he focused on Jack. "Been a long time, Jack. I heard about Mr. Mac. He was a good lawyer, if you can call lawyers good." His voice carried a wary edge.

"Mr. Jenkins? I'm Emmett Craig. I hope you don't mind talking to me. Mr. Mac left his case with me. I'd like to talk to you about your time at Whitaker Construction."

Jenkins stiffened. "That was a lifetime ago. Nothing to talk about."

Jack cut in. "Like I mentioned to you over the phone, this is about Darrell Boyd. Man's dying of cancer in prison for a crime some folks don't think he committed."

Jenkins checked his watch, then jerked his head toward a cluster of portable offices at the edge of the site. "I've got fifteen minutes before we start back up for the afternoon." He led them to a metal picnic table outside one trailer. Jenkins grabbed a cola from a nearby cooler and offered one to them. Emmett and Jack declined the drink but took a seat on the bench.

Jenkins took a long swig before giving them his attention. "Are you trying to get him out of prison? That place is certainly not for a dying man."

"No, it's not. We're revisiting the circumstances of James Whitaker's death," Emmett explained. "I understand you were let go from the company shortly before the murder."

Jenkins eyed him. "Fired. Let's call it what it was. Gave that company fourteen years of my life. James called me into his office and cut me loose."

Emmett leaned forward. "He didn't give a reason?"

"Officially? Budget cuts." Jenkins's laugh held no humor. "Unofficially? I asked too many questions about some of the company's business dealings."

Emmett exchanged a glance with Jack. "What questions?"

"Look, I was just a project manager. My job was to bring construction jobs in on time and under budget. But I noticed some irregularities in the material orders on River Pines. It was high-end condos." Jenkins took a sip from the can. "The numbers didn't add up."

"How so?" Jack prompted.

"We'd order, say, fifty pallets of premium marble tile at six hundred dollars a pallet. The invoices would show fifty, we'd get thirty delivered, but somehow full payment was approved." Jenkins's eyes hardened. "Multiply that across dozens of materials on multiple projects, and you're talking serious money disappearing."

"And you brought this to James's attention?"

"No, I originally brought it up to Darrell. Darrell was the COO. Darrell took it to James."

Emmett puzzled over Jenkins's response. "So you mainly talked to Darrell?"

Jenkins nodded. "Darrell brushed it off, said it had to be a bookkeeping error. But the 'errors' kept happening. So I started documenting everything. I took photos of deliveries, kept my own inventory records, and made copies of original orders versus what actually arrived. I presented those to Darrell, and he set up a meeting with James and his son, Alex."

Jack observed. "Alex? What exactly was his role?"

Jenkins smirked. "Good question. I guess he was some vice president or something. I know he started throwing his weight around. Even went over Darrell's head a few times. After that meeting, I was told they would look into the 'errors.' Instead, Alex started showing up at jobsites and meetings watching me like I was the one stealing or something. One day, I found him going through my files when I came back from lunch."

Emmett glanced at Jack, who shared a look. "Sounds like Alex became a bit of a pain."

Jenkins dropped his head. When he raised his face, his eyes were hard. "James was grooming his son to take over." Jenkins leaned forward. "But here's the thing. Alex had no skills. In fact, I got the impression he was pulling the wool over his dad and Darrell's eyes. Darrell wouldn't say anything, but Alex made him nervous too."

"Nervous how?" Emmett inquired.

"Well, James started leaving Darrell completely out of some projects, especially new acquisitions."

Emmett didn't want to interrupt, but he wondered if one of those projects was the one that supposedly led Whitaker to bankruptcy.

Jenkins continued. "Anyway, one day I was called into James's office. Alex was there too. James said they were downsizing because of financial difficulties and my position was being eliminated. Just like that. Keep in mind, I was a project manager, and we weren't quite finished with the condo project."

The bitterness in Jenkins's voice was palpable. "I lost my temper. Said some things I shouldn't have." Jenkins shook his head. "When James turned up dead, I knew the police would suspect me. But I was in Greenville with my sister the whole weekend. Security cameras at the hotel confirmed it."

"Did you tell the police about the financial discrepancies?"

"I did." Jenkins's face darkened. "Detective Simmons took my statement and all my documentation. Said he'd look into it. Next thing I know, Darrell's arrested."

Emmett frowned. "Your records established a potential motive for someone else."

"Exactly. But by then, they had their man. I hated Darrell taking the fall for James's murder. He was the most loyal guy. Even when it looked like James was pushing his son into the company, Darrell wasn't fazed. He loved what he did." Jenkins glanced at his watch. "Look, I need to get back. Anything else?"

"Just one thing," Emmett said. "Did you ever see James or Alex meeting with a man named Preston Langley?"

Jenkins's eyes grew wide, then narrowed as if he was making the connection between Emmett and Langley. If he did, Jenkins didn't mention it. Instead, he said, "I know who he is, but I never met him. James, and then Alex, did the wheeling and dealing behind closed-door meetings. I did ask Darrell about this big new project we all heard rumors about. Some fancy resort. It surprised me that the COO didn't know much about it."

"One last question," Emmett said. "Do you have copies of the documentation you collected? The photos, the inventory records?"

Jenkins scoffed. "After seven years? No, I turned everything over to the police during the investigation. Not that they seemed to care much. They already had their man."

"Thank you for your time, Mr. Jenkins," Emmett stood and extended his hand. "You've been extremely helpful."

Jenkins studied him for a moment before shaking his hand. "You really think Darrell didn't do it, don't you?"

"I do." Something caught Emmett's eye from the right. His gaze drifted past Jenkins toward a group of workers unloading materials from a truck. A familiar figure among the workers made his blood run cold.

Arnold Sullivan stood less than twenty-five feet away, watching them.

Jenkins followed Emmett's gaze. "You know him?"

Emmett swallowed hard. "Not directly. He's worked here long?"

Jenkins frowned. "Sullivan? He was here before me. Good worker, keeps to himself." He studied Emmett's face. "Problem?"

"No," Emmett looked away. "No problem. Thanks for your time, Mr. Jenkins."

Emmett and Jack headed back to the parking lot. Jack waited until they were out of earshot before speaking. "That's the brother of the victim in the Langley case, isn't it?"

Emmett blew out a breath, still feeling the man's stare on his back. "Arnold Sullivan? Yeah. And it's fine, I'm used to the stares." But he wasn't cool with the other stuff Arnold had been up to. Emmett was still convinced the man had been spending time outside his house and even tried to run him over with his truck.

Jack nudged. "So, here's my theory. Alex was embezzling from Whitaker Construction. James might have found out and confronted his son."

"Somebody was stealing money. But a son killing his father? I'm trying to wrap my head around it. Although, it's not like it hasn't happened before, and framing Darrell was almost too perfect."

Jack mused. "Langley has a history of violence that you know of personally. Do you think he's involved?"

Emmett paused by his car. "There are some parallels, if that's what you're asking. Langley was accused of killing his own business partner. But this is a completely different scenario."

Jack raised his eyebrow. "Is it?"

If Jack was trying to insinuate that Langley got away with murder thanks to him, Emmett needed to shut down his line of thinking. "This happened seven years ago. The charges against Langley were almost three years ago. What would his motive be?"

Jack shrugged. "Maybe James caught on to the fact that Langley had brought him a bogus project."

Emmett bit his lip. "It's something to look into."

"I can get on it if you want," Jack offered.

"Since I have history with Langley, I probably need to handle that personally."

"Understood, Counselor." Jack gave him a salute before climbing into his truck. Then he said, "Be careful. I've heard things about Langley. But you probably already know."

Emmett slid into his car and started the engine. He let the cool air blow across his face.

Yeah, he knew better than anyone to tread carefully around Langley.

He adjusted his rearview mirror, and the same figure caught his eye. Arnold Sullivan stood at the edge of the construction site, arms crossed, watching him with the same intensity he'd shown that day outside the courthouse. Thankfully, he made no move to approach.

Emmett gritted his teeth. Did Sullivan give Langley as much problem as he did him? He was starting to get really tired of the man.

He pulled away from the site, checking his mirrors until Sullivan's figure disappeared from his view.

Chapter 17

Sweetgrass Bed & Breakfast
Wednesday, May 21 at 3:35 p.m. EST

Yesterday's visit to see her father left Tracey emotionally drained and somehow lighter. Reconnecting with her father after so many years had loosened something long knotted inside her. She felt ashamed that she'd left town believing him capable of murder. Deep in her heart she didn't want it to be true. The crime never fit the affable man who'd raised her.

Thankfully, Jayden kept her busy. She put him to work helping Aunt Edna in the kitchen. As he did at home, he helped set ingredients on the counter and kept her aunt laughing as she cooked and baked. Tracey made sure to refresh the Robertson's room with clean sheets and towels. She missed this part of working in a bed-and-breakfast, making things comfortable for guests and getting to know them. The Robertsons were staying until the end of the week, and Tracey was delighted to hear that the older couple planned to visit again.

After vacuuming the Robertson's room, Tracey headed downstairs to see what her aunt was cooking up. The scent of apples and cinnamon met her at the kitchen door, as well as her son's excited voice asking questions.

Tracey stepped into the kitchen and hugged her son making him giggle. "Are you behaving yourself in here?"

"Yes." Jayden said in an exaggerated voice. "I'm helping Aunt E."

"Are you now? Aunt Edna, I forgot how much baking you do. What did you two make?"

Edna looked up and smiled. "This is something your mother used to make all the time. I ran across the recipe last night."

Jayden yelled. "Apple fritters!"

Tracey examined the golden brown lumps of deliciousness that lay cooling on a rack. "I remember these. These are my dad's favorite too. It's missing something, isn't it?"

Edna grinned. "I'm glad you remembered. Jayden, what does it need?"

He reached over and grabbed a silver shaker on the counter. "Powdered sugar! Can I add it?"

Aunt Edna clapped her hands together. "Go for it!"

Jayden went to shaking, probably adding a bit too much powdered sugar on some fritters.

Tracey gently touched his arm. "Okay, that's plenty."

Her son started laughing. "That was fun! Can I have one now? Are they still hot?"

"They should be cooled off now." Edna grabbed some plates and they all sat at the kitchen table to enjoy. Jayden went to his room to play his Nintendo Switch Lite. Last night, he insisted on trying Super Mario Odyssey. After reading through some things online, Tracey downloaded it for him. It was a change from his obsession with the Lego Marvel Superheroes.

"Everything okay?"

Tracey looked up to see her aunt's face overshadowed with concern. She tried smiling, "Yes."

Her aunt arched an eyebrow. "It's okay if it's not. I know yesterday was taxing for you. I'm glad Emmett went with you. Or should we be calling him Redd?" Edna gave her a sly smile as if she'd been clued into a secret.

Tracey laughed. "He doesn't seem to care. I definitely slipped up a few times yesterday and called him by his nickname. It's wonderful that he was able to get the medical transfer."

"Yes, God is good. After all of this, I'm hoping we can get my brother totally out of that place."

Tracey frowned. "I don't know if Emmett can prove anything after all this time, but I believe Dad."

"Good, that's good, Tracey. He needs you to believe in his innocence. Speaking of the transfer," Edna said. "I've been setting aside money every month since your daddy went to prison. For an appeal someday, I thought. But now..." She reached across the table to squeeze Tracey's hand. "We'll use it for his medical care. Whatever he needs that insurance doesn't cover."

Tracey felt tears prick her eyes. "Aunt Edna, you don't have to—"

"He's my baby brother," Edna said firmly. "And he's the only family I have left besides you and Jayden. Of course I'm going to help."

"Mom?" Jayden called out from the family room. "Aunt E? Is someone new coming to stay? There's a lady walking up to the porch."

Tracey and Edna exchanged glances. The bed-and-breakfast had no additional guests scheduled to arrive until the weekend.

"I hope it's not Lydia or Diane," Tracey muttered. Her shoulders tensed at the thought of another confrontation with Jayden's grandmother and aunt. But Jayden would have recognized either woman, so she set that thought aside.

Her aunt asked, "Tracey, do you mind going up front to see who it is? Sometimes I have people who drop-in wanting to find out more about Sweetgrass."

"Sure, I can do that."

When Tracey reached the door, her heart fluttered with fright. This was the last person she expected to see.

Wednesday, May 21 at 4:04 p.m. EST

Tracey stared in disbelief as she faced Helen Whitaker. The woman had aged considerably. Her blonde hair, more silver now, hung limply around a face lined with grief.

Tracey opened the door to greet her mother's oldest friend. They'd been roommates at the College of Charleston.

Helen stood on the threshold like a ghost from another time. Her expensive clothes draped loosely on her thin frame, and her once-sharp blue eyes seemed dull. She clutched a small handbag with both hands, her knuckles white with tension.

Helen's eyes settled on Tracey with an intensity that was unsettling. "You look so much like your mother," she whispered. "I'd forgotten how much."

Tracey stepped forward, unsure how to respond. "Mrs. Helen, what are you doing here? I mean, it's good to see you."

"I heard you were back. Word travels." Helen's voice trembled. "May I come in? Just for a moment?"

Tracey hesitated, then stepped aside. "Of course."

As Helen moved into the foyer, Tracey caught the faint scent of something medicinal beneath Helen's signature gardenia perfume. Helen's gaze darted around the entryway, taking in the familiar surroundings.

"It hasn't changed," she murmured. "Judith would be pleased. I miss your mother so much."

"Let's have a seat," Tracey suggested, guiding Helen into the front sitting room. Behind her, Tracey saw her aunt approaching, a stunned look on her face.

Helen sank into an armchair as if her legs could no longer support her weight. She peered up at Tracey with faint bruise-like shadows beneath her eyes.

Edna stepped into the room, her face blank. "Well, isn't this a surprise? Helen, it's been a long time. Can I get you something?" Not sure what to do, Tracey found it comforting that her aunt went into hostess mode.

Helen shook her head. "No, thank you. I... I just needed to see Tracey." She turned toward Tracey with a small smile. "When I heard you were back, I knew I had to come see Judith's daughter. It must have been awful for you. All of this."

The room fell silent. Tracey still wasn't sure how to react to Helen being here.

Helen's eyes filled with tears. "You lost your father. Because I couldn't..." She stopped, pressing her trembling hand to her mouth.

Edna stepped closer. "Helen, what are you saying?"

"I should have spoken up." A tear slipped down Helen's cheek. "James. Our marriage, it wasn't what people believed."

Did this woman know something that could have kept her father out of prison? Tracey exchanged a glance with her aunt, her heart racing. "Mrs. Whitaker, what do you mean? Spoken up about what?"

Helen's voice dropped to a whisper. "James and Alex argued terribly those last few weeks. I heard them shouting, and it broke my heart."

Edna reached out and grabbed Tracey's hand. They clutched each other's hand as if to keep each other upright.

"All I could think of was Judith. What would she have thought of them arresting Darrell?" Fresh tears spilled down her cheeks. "I should have said something. But Alex was so... so convincing. He said Darrell really killed James over the business."

Edna choked out. "Helen, what are you trying to say? After seven years?"

Helen looked directly at Tracey, her eyes suddenly clear. "Because Judith was my friend. Because I let her daughter suffer. Because Darrell is dying, and I can't let him die in prison for something he didn't do." She reached out a trembling hand toward Tracey. "I'm so sorry. Can you ever forgive me?"

Before Tracey could respond, the sound of tires on gravel outside caught their attention. Edna moved to the window and peered out. "It's Alex," she said, her voice tense. "And Rachel's with him."

Helen's face drained of color. "He must have realized I took the car. He tracks it, you know. Tracks me." She stood unsteadily. "I need to go. He will not be happy I came here."

Tracey rushed over, afraid the woman would topple over. "Miss Helen, do you need help? Is Alex—"

"Mom, there's a man outside." Jayden appeared in the doorway. "There sure are a lot of visitors today." His curious eyes moved from his mother to his aunt and then to Helen.

This was one time Tracey wished Jayden would remain glued to his game.

"Is that Judith's grandson?" Helen whispered, staring at Jayden.

"Yes. That's Jayden."

A sharp knock at the door made them all jump. "Mother?" Alex's angry voice called out. "I know you're in there."

Edna moved toward the door. "I'll handle this. Tracey, take Helen to the kitchen."

Tracey guided the trembling woman toward the back of the house, Jayden trailing behind them with wide eyes. They could hear the front door opening, Alex's voice rising, and Edna's calm response.

"Your son," Helen murmured, her hand reaching out toward Jayden but not quite touching him. "Does he know about his grandfather?"

"He will be visiting him soon," Tracey said, helping Helen into a chair at the kitchen table. "My dad's being transferred to Beaufort Memorial later this week."

Helen nodded. "That's good. Family should be together while they can."

Heavy footsteps approached the kitchen, and Alex appeared in the doorway, his face a mask of controlled rage. Rachel stood behind him.

What in the world was this?

Alex went straight over to Helen. "Mother, what are you doing here? You know the doctor said you shouldn't drive, not with your medication."

Helen's demeanor changed to an almost childlike confusion. "Alex? I got lost, I think. I was just having tea with Judith...no, with Tracey."

Alex's cold gaze shifted to Tracey, then to Jayden, who moved closer to his mother. "Did you encourage her to come here? She's not well. Hasn't been since my father was—" His eyes shifted again to Jayden, who now stood behind his mother, his own eyes wide.

Tracey appreciated Alex showing some sense, but the accusation in his tone was unmistakable. She placed a protective hand on Jayden's shoulder. "She came on her own, Alex. We were surprised to see her."

"I'm sure you were." His smile didn't reach his eyes. "Come, Mother. I'm taking you home."

Helen stood obediently, allowing Alex to take her arm. "I'm sorry for the trouble," she said. "It was... nice to see Judith's girl again. And her little boy."

Alex almost rolled his eyes, but seemed to catch himself. "Say goodbye, Mother."

"Goodbye, dears," Helen smiled.

Rachel stepped forward, placing a gentle hand on Helen's other arm. "I'll help get her settled in the car, Alex."

"No, I have her. You were supposed to watch her." Alex stared daggers at his sister.

As he guided Helen toward the front door, Rachel turned to Tracey. "I'm sorry about this. Mother's been confused lately. And the medication doesn't always help."

Tracey nodded, still stunned by the entire encounter. "It's okay. I was just surprised to see her."

They followed the others to the front door, watching as Alex helped Helen into the passenger seat of the Cadillac she must have driven over. A man in plain clothes got into the driver's seat of Helen's car, presumably to take it back to the Whitaker home.

Rachel called out to her brother. "Alex, I'll be there in a minute."

Alex gave his sister a hard look before climbing into his car. He sat there, engine running, staring at them all.

Rachel turned back to Tracey and Edna on the porch. "I'm mortified. Mother hasn't been herself lately. The doctors have adjusted her medication several times, but..." she trailed off, glancing back at the car where Helen sat staring vacantly ahead. "Did she say anything... unusual?"

Tracey hesitated and glanced at her aunt. "She mostly talked about my mother."

Rachel nodded, looking relieved. "Yes, she often confuses the past with the present. I'm sure it was overwhelming for you to see her like this."

Tracey admitted. "I'm sorry. I didn't know."

Rachel lowered her voice. "Look, I know our families have history. But I want you to know that I'm sorry about your father's illness. Alex... Well, he handles things his own way, but we're not all like that."

From the car, Alex honked the horn.

Rachel sighed. "I should go. Again, I apologize for the intrusion."

With that, she hurried to her car, leaving Tracey and Edna standing on the porch watching as the two vehicles pulled away.

Jayden tugged at his mother's sleeve. "Mom, why was that lady so sad?"

Tracey placed her hand on his head. "She's going through a hard time, sweetie. Why don't you go back and play your game? We'll have dinner soon."

After Jayden went inside, Tracey turned to her aunt. "What just happened?"

Edna shook her head, looking as confused as Tracey felt. They both returned inside and closed the door. Her aunt stood in the middle of the foyer, wringing her hands.

"Helen showing up here after all these years? I don't know what to think of it. Any of it."

Tracey lowered her voice, hoping Jayden had returned to the family room. "Did you notice how frightened Helen seemed when Alex arrived? Her behavior was strange anyway, but then she changed. She seemed almost normal one minute, talking about how she should have spoken up, and then confused the next. What do you think she meant about James and Alex arguing?"

Edna narrowed her eyes. "I don't know, but something ain't right with that family. And Rachel hanging back to apologize?"

Tracey crossed her arms. "I think she was just trying to find out what her mother said."

Edna nodded. "Probably. The Whitakers have always been good at keeping up appearances. But cracks are showing. Helen wouldn't have come here without a reason, confused or not." She headed to the kitchen. "I was about to check on the food in the oven before we were so rudely interrupted by the Whitakers."

Tracey followed her aunt into the kitchen. "Did you hear what I heard? Helen said she should have spoken up at the trial. That she's been carrying this guilt all these years. And her children tracked her here."

Edna pulled a pan of biscuits out of the oven before responding. "It seems crazy, but maybe she has gotten lost enough for them to keep a tracker on her."

"I guess. Do you think Helen knows something about James's murder? Something that could help my dad?"

Edna placed the biscuits on a rack to cool. "I don't know, baby girl. But if Helen is trying to ease her conscience after all these years, maybe Emmett needs to know about this visit."

Tracey nodded. "Let me call him."

The Whitakers had a lot of influence in this town, but they were clearly hiding something.

God, let all their secrets spill out into the light.

Chapter 18

Emmett paced his living room with his phone pressed to his ear as he listened to Tracey.

"Redd, she just showed up. No warning. We don't know if she was trying to tell us something. It felt like she was. Then Alex and Rachel showed up. You could feel the rage rolling off that man. He had the nerve to accuse us of asking Helen to come. And Rachel... She was just as weird to me. You gotta look into the Whitakers. Something is not right."

He wanted so badly to share his suspicions. But he needed to tread softly and carefully. Emmett stopped at the window, peering into the growing darkness as if he might spot lurking dangers. It was more of what was in his mind than outside.

Tracey was clearly rattled, so he was too. Then he thought about Jayden. "Tracey, where was Jayden during all of this?"

She sucked in a breath that almost sounded like a sob to him. "My curious child. He's not used to being around this amount of people. Everything has fascinated him about this whole trip. I told him to go play his game, but he was right there. He told me Alex scared him, but he felt bad for Helen. He keeps talking about the sad lady."

Remembering how friendly the little boy was when he arrived, Emmett slapped his hand against his forehead. Now he felt protective of Jayden too. He was way too young to be exposed to this stuff.

Tracey continued as if still processing. "She came over here completely out of the blue. But why? I know she was good friends with my mother. But mom's been gone for twenty years. Helen didn't come around like that when James died and my dad was accused of murder."

Emmett nudged. "What exactly was she trying to tell you? I've been told she's a recluse. I assumed she had a mental breakdown of some sort when James died."

"She definitely wasn't the same woman I remembered. I wondered if she'd been drinking. I thought I smelled alcohol. But she was almost lucid one minute and then confused the next. Emmett, she said things like she should have come forward. She has something locked in her brain that's bothering her."

"Did she mention anything else?"

"She said she should have spoken up at the trial," Tracey continued. "That she's been carrying this guilt for years.

Then Alex showed up and it was like watching her transform into a completely different person. He practically dragged her out of here."

"Alex must have been tracking her to know how to find her. That's concerning." Emmett sat heavily on his couch. "Listen, Tracey, I got word that the transfer will happen on Friday for your father. I'm thinking your father's illness and this transfer could be shaking up some things."

"Sounds like it. What's our next move in the investigation? Helen's visit has to mean something."

Emmett hesitated, wrestling with how much to share. Jack's discovery from the bank records about possible embezzlement and Langley's connection was too explosive for even him. He needed more information.

He decided to tell her what he knew for sure. "I'm following several leads. Former employees of Whitaker Construction who might have seen things. Bank records that don't quite add up. I should have more concrete information in a few days."

"You're still holding something back, aren't you?" The directness of her question caught him off guard. "Please tell me you're looking at the Whitakers too. You heard what I just told you."

He closed his eyes, pinching the bridge of his nose beneath his glasses. "Tracey, there are aspects of this case that are... complicated. I'm being careful about how we proceed for legal purposes."

"My father doesn't have time for careful," she reminded him, a new edge in her voice. "And I'm not some fragile flower who needs protecting from the truth."

"I know you're not," he said softly. "You're one of the strongest people I've ever met. But knowing certain things could put you and Jayden at risk, and I—" He stopped himself, realizing he was about to say more than he should.

"You what?" she prompted.

"I couldn't live with myself if something happened to either of you because of this case," he finished honestly. He had created enemies when he defended Langley. Emmett wasn't all that sure if his own client wasn't a danger to him. They both knew Langley had been guilty of murder.

The silence that followed felt weighted. He was almost afraid Tracey had hung up on him. That's not what he wanted. She needed to know he was doing everything he could.

When Tracey spoke again, her tone had softened. "I appreciate that, Emmett. I do. But this is my family we're talking about. My father. I need to know what we're facing."

"Soon," he promised. "Let me nail down a few more details first. For now, let's focus on getting your father transferred. That's the immediate priority."

She sighed. "Fine. So it's definitely going to be Friday?"

"I've been in contact with the prison medical staff and Beaufort Memorial. Everything is ready to go."

"Will you be there?"

The vulnerability in her request tugged at something in his chest. "Of course," he said without hesitation. "I'm happy to drive you over to the hospital too. Do you think you'll bring Jayden?"

She paused before responding. "I'm not sure. Part of me thinks he should meet his grandfather while there's still time, but another part of me..."

"It's a difficult decision. There's no right or wrong answer."

Tracey let out a tremulous breath. "I want to see how Dad is settling in, what the environment is like. Make sure it won't be too overwhelming for an eight-year-old."

"That makes sense." Emmett leaned back against the couch cushions. He was grateful their conversation had turned back natural as if they'd known each other for years rather than being re-acquainted only days ago. He knew Tracey reached out to him to look more into the Whitakers, but she'd easily confided in him as if she trusted him.

"Emmett?" Her voice pulled him from his thoughts. "Are you still there?"

"Sorry, yes," he said, straightening. "Just thinking about the case."

"I was just saying I appreciate you."

He was glad they were on the phone and she couldn't see the huge grin on his face. "I'm happy to be there for you and your family. I'll call you tomorrow with the transfer schedule."

They said their goodbyes, and Emmett sat in the quiet of his living room, phone still in hand. The investigation was accelerating, and connections between Langley, Alex, and the Whitaker Construction Company seemed impossible to ignore.

Why did Helen go see Tracey today? Had the mother been hiding something all this time about her son? That would explain Alex's belligerent behavior. Maybe he was scared about someone discovering his involvement in his dad's murder.

Emmett looked at the time on his phone. It was close to nine o'clock. He and Tracey had talked for almost an hour. He wished he'd caught her messages earlier before he arrived home. He would have preferred to go over to Sweetgrass and discuss that kind of news in person. But they would see each other on Friday, which would likely be a long day.

He rubbed his forehead. This was his client's daughter. What was wrong with him thinking about spending time with her? Emmett shook his head; he needed to get his brain back working in the right direction again.

Seeing his phone in his hand, he had a thought and made a call.

"Daniels."

"Hey, Jack, it's Emmett. I have a new development." He explained to the private detective about Helen's visit to the bed-and-breakfast along with her children coming to get her.

Jack commented. "Now, that's interesting. So what are you thinking?"

"I think this confirms Mr. Mac's note about the Whitakers. Apparently, something is breaking apart."

Jack chuckled. "Secrets. People can't keep things hidden from the light like they want. I got another partner I can call on to look into the mother and sister. I'll follow Alex myself."

Emmett warned. "Just as long as he doesn't recognize you."

"Counselor, I'm no amateur. Believe me, Alex will never know that I'm there. You watch your back. People can get a little antsy when they think their time is up."

"Don't worry. I can take care of myself."

Jack laughed heartily. "I bet you can. I will be in touch."

Emmett clicked off the phone call and switched to his security camera out of habit. He frowned. Looked like his stalker was back.

Did this Sullivan guy not have anything better to do?

Chapter 19

Tracey discussed an idea with her Aunt Edna on Thursday. She wasn't even sure why she'd thought about it and probably wouldn't have except Edna thought it best for Tracey to be with her father first.

"You're his sister? I would think you'd want to be there."

"Believe me I would love to, but I have visited with Darrell many, many times over the years. He wants you there. Besides, the Robertsons are checking out Friday morning. Then I need to strip down the room and clean for the next guests."

While her aunt felt like she could keep up with Jayden, Tracey knew her child. "We're going to be here at least another week. I want Dad to settle in before Jayden sees him." She shouldn't have felt guilty, but when Lydia and Diane came by on Sunday, she realized how much Jayden wanted to know more about his father. "I think I'm going to see if Jayden can visit with his grandmother."

Her aunt Edna shook her head. "Tracey, are you sure you're not putting too much trust in Lydia?"

"When we return to Florida, I don't know when we'll be back. So far I haven't heard from Regina, but I know she has to be itching for my return. Besides, I'm not going to be that far away."

Still, if Tracey were honest, her anxiety was on ten. Not only was her father finally getting the care he needed, she was letting Jordan's mother spend time with his son.

Jayden was ecstatic. Tracey had kept him cooped up at the bed-and-breakfast and really hadn't given him a chance to explore her hometown.

"You have my cell number," Tracey said, handing the neatly written note to Lydia, "and Aunt Edna's number is on this paper too." She fought to keep her voice steady, to not let her anxiety show as Jayden explored the living room of his father's childhood home.

"Tracey, honey, we've got this," Lydia assured her, tucking the paper into her pocket with a patient smile. "I really appreciate this. Jayden will have had a wonderful day with his grandmother and aunt."

"I know." Tracey watched as Jayden studied a shelf of trophies in the corner. Tracey was familiar with the basketball and track awards bearing Jordan's name. Her son's eyes widened with fascination, hungry for these connections to the father he barely remembered.

Lydia followed her gaze. "He looks so much like his daddy."

Tracey needed to leave before she changed her mind. "If you don't mind, I'll call to check in around lunchtime."

"You focus on your father," Lydia said. "Let us take some of the burden off your shoulders."

A car horn honked outside. Emmett had been gracious, driving her to drop off Jayden before they headed to the hospital.

"Jayden," Tracey called. "I'm leaving now. Come give me a hug."

Her son bounded over. "Mom, tell Grandpa I will see him soon."

Tracey kneeled, taking his face between her hands. "Be good, okay? Listen to Grandma Lydia. I'll call later to check on you."

"I will." He hugged her quickly and ran back to the couch where a stack of photo albums sat on the coffee table.

With a final glance at Jayden, already absorbed in a photo album, Tracey turned to leave. Her heart felt like she was leaving her son behind, reminding her of the first time she'd dropped him off at daycare and later, his first day of school. This was almost too big for her to process.

The morning air was thick with humidity, promising another scorching day. Emmett waited in his car in the Harris's driveway, sunglasses on, window down. Something about his steady presence calmed her racing thoughts.

"Are you okay?" he asked as she slid into the passenger seat.

"Yeah." She fastened her seatbelt, forcing herself not to look back at the house.

Emmett navigated the car down the street. "The hospital called this morning. The transfer went smoothly, and he's settled in."

"Thanks to you." She meant it. She knew Emmett had worked through the night coordinating with the prison, the hospital, and the transport team to make sure nothing went wrong. "I don't think I've properly thanked you for everything you've done."

His eyes remained on the road, but red marks creeped up around his cheeks. "Just doing my job."

Tracey rolled her eyes jokingly. "So modest! You've gone above and beyond for my father. For all of us."

Emmett pulled into the parking lot of Beaufort Memorial. "Mind if I ask you something?"

"Go ahead."

"What's waiting for you in Panama City?"

The question caught her off guard. "My job," she said slowly. "Jayden's school."

"Do you like it there? Your job, I mean."

"It used to be great. My boss, Lauren, was amazing—like a mentor. But she retired, and her niece Regina took over."

She hesitated. "It's not the same now. My boss is entitled, demanding, and completely lacks empathy. But the pay is good, and Jayden loves his school."

He finally removed his sunglasses. "How has it felt to be back here?"

She stared into his eyes. Up close, they were hazel but seemed to be more green in the sunlight. "There have been some moments. Working with Aunt Edna at Sweetgrass this week reminded me how much I missed the bed-and-breakfast. How it was when my mother was still alive and they first started the Sweetgrass." She knew they were killing time sitting in the car, but she didn't feel bad about it. "What about you? How did you end up back in Beaufort?"

Emmett was quiet for a moment. "My father died two years ago. We weren't close. He had a bit of a drinking problem most of my life."

"I'm sorry. I remember kids talking."

He shrugged. "When he died, I inherited the house. I came back to sell it, actually. But being back here felt right, somehow. Mr. Mac convinced me it wasn't a bad idea to stay."

"I always thought you felt at home at the Macs."

"Yeah, I really did, but maybe we can talk about that later." He gazed at her as if he was studying every part of her face. "Your dad is waiting. Are you ready to go in?"

She smiled. "Yes, I think so."

Earlier, Emmett had said he was only doing his job. But Tracey realized as they headed to the hospital entrance that once again, he'd eased her anxiety. A simple conversation with him grounded her for what was ahead.

Beaufort Memorial Hospital
Friday, May 23 at 10:00 a.m. EST

They approached the hospital wing where prisoner-patients were kept. Outside Room 412, a corrections officer in a gray uniform straightened in his chair. "Visiting Darrell Boyd?" His voice was professionally neutral.

"Yes," Emmett produced his ID. "Emmett Craig, his attorney. And this is his daughter, Tracey Boyd."

The officer checked their names against a clipboard. "I'll need to see your ID as well, ma'am."

Tracey handed over her driver's license, feeling like she was back at the prison despite the hospital's sterile hallway and antiseptic smell.

"Any gifts or personal items need to be inspected," the officer said, eyeing the small bag Tracey carried.

"Just some family photos to put by his bed," she explained, opening the bag to show him.

The officer nodded after a cursory inspection. "Thirty minutes. I'll be right here the whole time." He knocked twice on the door before opening it for them.

When they entered the hospital room, the difference from the medical ward at the prison was stark. Sunlight streamed through actual windows, flowers brightened a bedside table, and her father rested against clean white pillows. Though still gaunt, some of the tension had eased from his face.

His eyes lit up when he saw her. "Tracey."

"Dad." She moved to his side, taking his hand. It was good to see her father in a real hospital, receiving proper care at last.

"You came," he said, as if he doubted she would. "Where's Jayden?"

"He's spending the day with Jordan's family." She pulled out the framed photo she had of Jayden's second grade year. "I thought it would be good for him to learn more about his father."

Darrell's face clouded. "The Harrises? Are you sure that's wise after what they tried to do?"

Tracey blinked. "You know about the custody battle?"

"Of course. Edna told me," he said. "My sister didn't keep much from me. Why would you leave him with people who tried to take him from you?"

"They're his family too," Tracey said. "Here's his most recent school photo. Would you like to see?"

Her father grinned. "Yea, let me look at my handsome grandson."

"He's quite a talker." Tracey looked back at Emmett watching them. "Redd... I mean Emmett has seen Jayden in action."

Emmett grinned. "He's definitely very inquisitive and loves Spider-Man."

Darrell laughed, "Well, I'm looking forward to seeing him all grown-up. I take it your aunt is busy with Sweetgrass."

"Yes, she's prepping for some new guests this weekend, but she will be here soon."

Emmett stepped forward. "I'm going to step out and make a few phone calls. Mr. Boyd, I wanted to make sure you're being treated alright."

"Everything is fine. I'm just happy to be out of that place." He looked over at Tracey. "And seeing my daughter."

After Emmett left, Tracey pulled up the chair next to her father's bed. She grabbed her dad's hand. "I hope they can make you comfortable."

"Oh, I'm feeling good right now."

Tracey felt her phone vibrate. "Sorry, I need to take a look. It might be Jayden." She pulled out the phone and glimpsed the screen. It was an email notification from Regina.

URGENT: Southeast Banking Updates Needed.

Below was a missed call notification from Regina. She wasn't sure how she'd missed the call, but Regina would have to wait. Tracey slipped her phone back into her purse with a slight eye roll.

Her father noticed the gesture. "Everything alright?"

"Just my boss," Tracey said. "All her issues are emergencies."

Her father's eyes clouded with concern. "You shouldn't lose your job over me, Tracey."

"I won't." She reached for his hand. "My boss's father approved my leave. Regina... she's used to getting her way." Tracey attempted to smile. "She can wait. This is more important."

There was a gentle knock at the door. Tracey thought it might be Emmett returning, but a tall man with salt-and-pepper hair and wire-rimmed glasses entered carrying a tablet.

"Mr. Boyd, how are we feeling this afternoon?" His accent carried hints of his Indian heritage. "Ah, visitors. Hello, I'm Dr. Patel."

Darrell introduced her. "Dr. Patel, this is my daughter, Tracey."

Dr. Patel's expression warmed. "It's a pleasure to meet you, Ms. Boyd."

"Likewise." Tracey nodded. "Thank you for taking care of him. What happens next?"

Dr. Patel looked down at his tablet before addressing them. "We've run initial blood work and completed a new set of scans this morning," he explained. "The cancer has progressed significantly since his last evaluation at the prison. It's spread to his liver and lungs."

Tracey gently squeezed her father's hand.

Dr. Patel continued. "At this stage, our focus is palliative care. That means we want to keep your father comfortable and maintain his quality of life for as long as possible."

"How long?" Darrell asked.

Dr. Patel met his gaze directly. "It's difficult to be precise."

"Is there nothing else that can be done?" Tracey asked, fighting to keep her voice steady. "No treatments or—"

"We could try a mild chemotherapy regimen," Dr. Patel said, "but in your father's weakened state, the side effects would likely outweigh any potential benefits. That said, I believe in patient choice. If you wanted to try—"

"No," Darrell interrupted. "I just want whatever time I have left to be worth something." He looked at Tracey. "To spend it with my family."

Dr. Patel nodded. "I understand. We'll focus on pain management and keeping you comfortable. My team will be monitoring you closely, and I'll stop by each morning." He bowed his head. "I'll give you some time with your daughter, but a nurse will be in shortly with medication."

Tracey noticed how intently her father was looking at her. "Are you okay? Do you want me to get the nurse?"

He shook his head. "Not yet. Once she gives me that medicine, I'll be knocked out. You look so much like your mother."

That made Tracey think of Helen's strange visit. She didn't want to think about the Whitakers right now. Instead, she and her dad talked about her job back in Florida until the nurse came. Tracey glanced at her phone and realized her time was up. She slipped out feeling regretful at how quickly the thirty minutes had past.

Emmett was down the hall sitting in the waiting room. "How's everything going?"

She told him what Dr. Patel said. "They're just going to keep him comfortable."

"I'm sorry, Tracey."

She wiped her eyes. "I should check on Jayden." She dialed Lydia's number. Hearing her son's voice was exactly what she needed. Instead, the phone rang repeatedly before going to voicemail.

"That's odd," she murmured, ending the call. "Let me try Diane's cell."

Again, no answer. A tendril of worry snaked through her chest. She checked the time. 12:30. She told Lydia she would call around lunch.

Emmett touched her arm, his eyes boring into her. "What's wrong?"

"Lydia isn't answering." She tried Lydia's number again with the same result. "She knew I'd be calling around lunchtime."

He suggested. "Maybe they're out somewhere? A restaurant with bad reception?"

"Maybe," Tracey didn't think so. Was this a mistake? Why didn't she just bring Jayden with her to the hospital? She sensed Emmett watching her. He probably thought she was an overprotective mom.

"Try Edna," he suggested. "Maybe she's heard from them."

"That's a good idea." Before Tracey could dial, her phone rang. Lydia's number flashed on the screen. "Lydia?" Tracey answered quickly. "I've been trying to reach you."

"I'm so sorry." Lydia's voice crackled through the line. "We were out in the backyard. Jayden was practicing free throws just like his father used to do. I'm still not used to this smartphone Diane got me. I didn't hear it ringing, and then I realized the battery was nearly dead."

Tracey closed her eyes, exhaling slowly. "Can I talk to Jayden, please?"

"Of course. He's right here." There was a rustling sound, then her son's excited voice came through.

"Mom! Guess what? Grandma Lydia showed me Dad's basketball hoop! It's still here, and I made three shots in a row!"

Tracey smiled. "That's great, sweetie."

"But I'm kinda ready to go back to Aunt E's now," Jayden added, his voice dropped almost to a whisper. "Grandma Lydia keeps showing me more and more pictures and telling me stories, and it's cool but... I miss my games, and Aunt E said she was making cookies this afternoon."

"I'll be back soon and we can go home to Aunt E's. Are you having lunch?"

"Yeah, Grandma Lydia made PB&J sandwiches. They're okay."

Tracey laughed softly. "I love you, Jayden."

"Love you too, Mom! How's Grandpa?"

"He's resting right now. But he can't wait to see you. Let me talk to Grandma Lydia again, okay?"

Tracey stood and walked over to the other side of the waiting room. Her anxiety had built up so she couldn't sit still.

Lydia came back on the line. "I hope we've put your mind at ease. We're taking good care of him."

"Do you have any idea how terrified I was?" Tracey's voice shook. Her fears had morphed into anger. "I called three times, Lydia. Three times with no answer."

"I told you, we were in the backyard—"

"I was afraid something had happened to my son," Tracey cut her off. "The same son you tried to take away from me. The same son I left here with because of what you did."

There was a heavy silence on the line. When Lydia spoke again, her voice was subdued. "You're right to be angry. I didn't think—"

"No, you didn't think. Just like you didn't think about what I was going through all those years ago, losing Jordan and then having my father arrested. You saw an opportunity and took it, trying to use my pain against me to get custody."

"Tracey..." Lydia's voice cracked. "I made a terrible mistake back then. I was so consumed by grief over losing Jordan that I couldn't see straight. I thought I was doing what was best for Jayden, but I was wrong."

The raw emotion in the older woman's voice caught Tracey off guard. She wasn't sure how she felt.

"I've had five years to regret what I did," Lydia continued. "Five years, watching you raise that boy from a distance through the few photos Edna shared. And you know what? You've done a remarkable job. Jayden is kind, smart, and curious. Jordan would be proud. I'm proud of you."

Tracey found herself speechless. The anger that had been fueling her dissipated. Instead, tears pooled at the edges of her eyes.

"I'm not asking for your forgiveness," Lydia said. "I'm just asking for a chance to be in his life, however you see fit. On your terms."

"I appreciate that, Lydia. I'll be there in a bit to pick up Jayden." She ended the call and wiped her eyes. All of a sudden, she felt so exhausted. Behind her, she sensed a presence. Tracey turned slightly to find Emmet standing nearby.

With worry on his face, he stepped up and touched her arm. "Is everything okay? Do you want me to take you to pick up Jayden?"

Tracey wiped her eyes, feeling comforted that her father's lawyer was ready to do battle for her. For a moment, she thought about wrapping her arms around him. He was so close and his touch, his voice were all soothing.

She caught her breath and swept away the thought. "Everything's okay. They were just in the backyard."

Emmett continued to hold her arm. "Are you sure?"

She nodded, liking the warmth of his hand on her arm. "I hate to treat you like a chauffeur, but Jayden is ready to go back to Aunt E's."

"I'm ready when you are."

Tracey looked down the hallway. "Can I check on Dad before we leave? I'm assuming the guard will remember me."

"It should be fine. Your dad will probably be sleeping for a while with the medication," Emmett reminded her.

Walking toward her father's room, Tracey felt the tension easing from her shoulders. At least Jayden was safe.

The guard looked up as she approached.

"I just want to say goodbye, if that's okay."

The guard gave her a sharp nod. "That's fine."

She peeked in on her father, who seemed to be sleeping peacefully. Her eyes watered remembering her mother in a similar situation twenty years ago. That dreaded "C" word had already stolen one parent from her, and now it would take the other.

She stepped back out of the room and turned toward Emmett. He smiled down at her. Somehow his smile made her feel like everything was going to be alright. She was a bit surprised at her desire to be hugged by him. When he'd touched her arm earlier, that too had felt good. She knew he was going beyond what he was supposed to be doing professionally.

On their way back to his car, she spoke up. "I feel like I'm taking advantage of your kindness. You're my dad's lawyer."

He stopped and stared at her. The look he gave her made her feel like she was the only one in the world he cared about. "I'd like to think that we're rekindling a past friendship. I'm the kind of guy that is there for people he cares about. Is that okay with you?"

Tracey nodded, overwhelmed and pleased by his answer.

Out of everything she'd encountered coming back home, Emmett Craig was not what she'd expected at all.

Chapter 20

Memorial Day Weekend
Saturday, May 24 at 3:01 p.m. EST

Tracey hadn't realized that Memorial Day was upon them. She thought about how busy the Morrison would be this weekend and for the rest of the summer. For a bed-and-breakfast, her aunt wasn't doing too bad with the Sweetgrass either.

While her aunt prepared a meal, Tracey helped check in their guests. Three older women chatted like they were young girls in the sitting room. Though the group was staying until Tuesday, they had enough luggage between them for two weeks. With three bedrooms upstairs, their stay placed the bed-and-breakfast at capacity.

"The blue room has the best morning light, Ms. Carter. And you'll find fresh towels in the en-suite bathroom."

"Please, call me Laura." The silver-haired woman wore her thick framed cat glasses on the edge of her nose.

"We've been doing these getaways for thirty years now, but this is our first time in Beaufort."

"Well, you picked a beautiful weekend to visit," Tracey said, handing over the key. "The weather is perfect for exploring the waterfront."

The tallest of the three women, who had introduced herself as Meredith, chimed in. "It smells so good in here. We're excited about the homecooked meal. What's on the menu?"

"My aunt is making her famous shrimp gumbo. You'll love it." Tracey looked down and handed Meredith the key to the yellow room.

"Ooh, I can't wait. I'm starving." The third woman, Patricia, clutched a guidebook to her chest.

Tracey grinned as she handed Patricia the green room key. "Please help yourself to snacks and coffee." She pointed to the snack bar she'd filled up at lunch. She'd brewed fresh coffee right before their arrival.

The front door opened, and Tracey looked up to see Charlene stepping into the foyer. Her box braids were pulled up on the top of her head in a bun. "Sorry," she said with a small wave, "didn't mean to interrupt."

"Not at all," Tracey replied. "Speaking of friends, ladies, this is my best friend. Charlene, these are our guests for the weekend."

"Nice to meet y'all," Charlene grinned. "Girls' weekend?"

"Forty years of friendship and counting," Diane stated.

Meredith laughed. "We were roommates in college."

"That's wonderful," Charlene replied. "Tracey and I go way back too, though not quite that far yet. We're more like twenty years."

The women thanked Tracey and headed upstairs with their bags. As soon as they were out of earshot, Charlene crossed the room and pulled Tracey into a tight hug.

"How are you holding up? Your aunt has you working?"

Tracey exhaled deeply. "I actually volunteered. The work is good for me. It's been hard seeing my dad."

Charlene nodded. "I know, that's why I'm here. How is he?"

"I'll fill you in. Let's head to the family room. I need to get off my feet."

On the way through the kitchen, Charlene went over to hug Edna. "Auntie, you got it smelling good in here. And, Jayden, what are you doing?"

Jayden sat at the table with his coloring books. "I was helping, but I don't like touching the shrimp. They look funny."

They all laughed.

"Aunt Edna, let me know if you need any help," Tracey said.

Her aunt waved her hand. "I'm fine. Jayden will help me set the table in a bit. He's learning quite a bit about the family business."

Tracey and Charlene sat down on the couch in the family room. She tried to tell Charlene all she could remember. "Dr. Patel gave us the rundown. The cancer's spread to Dad's liver and lungs."

"Oh, Trace..." Charlene grabbed her hand.

"They offered chemotherapy, but Dad refused." Tracey's voice caught. "He said he just wants to spend whatever time he has left with family."

"How do you feel about that?"

"I don't know," Tracey admitted. "Part of me wants him to fight, but another part understands. He's tired."

"Has Jayden seen him yet?"

Tracey shook her head. "Not yet. I will take Jayden to see him tomorrow after church."

The sharp trill of her phone cut through the air. Tracey glanced at the screen and groaned. "It's my boss."

Charlene's mouth dropped open. "On the weekend! She has some nerve. Don't answer it, Tracey."

"I've been ignoring her emails and phone calls since yesterday. She's not going to stop. I looked at the emails from Mia, and it's not even that serious." Tracey took a deep breath and swiped to accept the call. "Hello, Regina."

"Tracey. Finally, I was just checking my calendar. Do you think you will come back this week?"

Tracey stiffened. "My father just started palliative care yesterday. I'll need another week to get him settled."

The pause on the line stretched uncomfortably. "Palliative care?"

Tracey's stomach knotted. "Yes, I didn't realize his illness was more serious. I've been working remotely. Is there something specific you need?"

Regina's voice sounded strained. "I'm sorry to hear about the circumstances, but what are we going to do? It really helps when you're here in person at meetings."

Tracey frowned. "I mentioned I would need at least two weeks. And I have the leave."

"Are you sure it will only be two weeks? I mean with your father..."

"Everything is unpredictable right now, Regina."

Regina's voice switched to a whine. "It's just that you weren't available yesterday. I scrambled to figure out how to finish the report. Mia wasn't much help. I hoped you would be back after Memorial Day."

Tracey felt her fury rising. "Mr. Morrison told me, when he approved my leave, that I could take as much time as I needed. Should I reach out to him?"

After a frosty silence, Regina finally said. "We'll discuss your return date at another time." Then the line went dead before Tracey could respond.

Charlene clapped slowly, a grin spreading across her face. "Sounds like you stood up for yourself. It's about time."

Tracey put her hand over her forehead. "Girl, I still need that job."

Charlene countered. "Do you really? Tracey, your skills are transferrable. You can go anywhere."

"I don't know what I want anymore," Tracey whispered. "I haven't been happy at the Morrison since my old boss left. Regina makes my job miserable."

Charlene squeezed her hand. "So maybe you don't leave."

"What? Stay in Beaufort?"

"Your dad needs you. You need him." Charlene eyed her. "Plus, I know you want to clear your father's name."

"I'm no lawyer." A smile tugged at Tracey's lips. "That's what Redd is doing."

"Oooh, I see that smile," Charlene teased. "I know this is a difficult time for you. You need to enjoy this time with your father. Believe me, when my dad died, it all happened so fast."

"I'm so sorry." Tracey reached over and hugged her friend. "It's hard losing your parents."

Charlene let out a breath. "Yeah, it is, girl." She tilted her head, listening to the voices above them. "You have quite the guests this weekend. Sounds like they're going to have a good time."

That was one disadvantage of staying on the bottom floor of a full bed-and-breakfast. "Yeah, must be nice to get away and have some fun."

Her friend lifted a finger to her chin. "I have an idea."

Tracey knew that look. "Oh no! Girl, what are you thinking?"

"Well, my brother is over at Emmett's house. He's helping him out with renovations. We should drop by to see how things are looking."

"Why?" Tracey arched an eyebrow. "I mean, I did mention to Redd that I wouldn't mind seeing what's he's doing with the place."

Charlene smacked her arm. "Perfect!"

"Ouch!" Tracey rubbed her arm.

"We need to get you out of the house. We haven't done anything together since you've been here."

Tracey looked around. "Someone needs to watch Jayden. I can't put that on Aunt Edna."

"We can take him over to hang out at Kenny's house with his boys. What do you think?"

Tracey thought about it. "He hasn't been around anyone his age. I guess it wouldn't hurt."

"Good. That means we get you both out of the house. I know your aunt appreciates you being here, but this town is your home."

Her friend was right. This was home.

But could she really stay here?

Chapter 21

Beaufort, South Carolina
Saturday, May 24 at 5:17 p.m. EST

Emmett stood back to assess their handiwork, wiping sweat from his brow with his forearm. The newly opened space between the kitchen and living room transformed the old house, casting afternoon light through areas that had been dim and closed off when his father lived here.

"Man, it's already a different place," Kenny said, gathering sawdust into a pile with a wide push broom. His powerful frame made the work look effortless. "Your daddy would never recognize it now."

Emmett chuckled as he ran his hand along the exposed beam they'd installed to support the ceiling where the wall had been. "Needed to make it mine, you know?"

Kenny nodded. "I hear that. Though I'm still not sold on this 'open concept' business. Feels like TV designer talk."

"Says the man who builds houses for a living."

"I build 'em traditional. Walls where walls should be." Kenny grinned. "But I'll admit, it looks good."

The sound of tires on gravel drifted through the open windows. Emmett glanced out to see a car pulling into the driveway. Not Jack's pickup. He was looking to hear from the private detective. With Darrell officially receiving palliative care, he wanted to clear the man's name before he left this world.

When he saw who it was, his heart leaped in his chest.

"Is that my sister?" Kenny asked, moving to stand beside Emmett at the window. He let out a low whistle. "And Tracey, too. What'd you do to deserve this house call?"

He didn't know, but he was pleasantly surprised as he watched Tracey and Charlene make their way up the front walk. Tracey wore jeans and a simple blue top. He enjoyed seeing her curls loose.

"I mentioned the renovations," he admitted. "She said she'd like to see what I was doing with the place." Suddenly, he looked down at his jeans and t-shirt, both filthy with sawdust. Not his usual suit and tie attire.

Kenny shot him a look. "Uh-huh. Is it me or have you spent an awful amount of time with Ms. Tracey?"

Warmth spread across his face. "It's been a busy week."

Kenny clasped his shoulder and started laughing. "Whatever you say, man."

The doorbell rang. Emmett checked his reflection in a nearby mirror and grimaced. He had sawdust in his hair, and a smudge of drywall compound on his cheek.

When he opened the door, Charlene burst out laughing. "Well, if it isn't Bob, I mean Redd the Builder. You trying to leave the law and join my brother in construction?"

Tracey stood behind her, a smile played on her lips. "I told Charlene we should have called first."

"No, it's fine," Emmett ran a hand through his hair. "We're just finishing up for the day. Come in."

They stepped inside, and Tracey's eyes widened. "Oh wow. I take it there was a wall there at one time."

He grinned. "Yeah! I had a lot of fun tearing it down."

She moved further into the room and spun around. "It was a great idea. I imagine you get a lot more sunlight through that front window and then from the windows in the kitchen."

"Oh yeah. The living room was a pretty dreary place." Emmett recalled the old, dark furniture his dad kept in the living space, including a well-worn recliner. He'd tossed the old blinds and replaced them with modern shades.

Charlene headed straight for the kitchen and perused his refrigerator. "Redd, what kind of eating do you be doing? This fridge has nothing but takeout containers and condiments."

Kenny came from the back of the house. Emmett noticed his friend had attempted to wash his face, but still had sawdust in his hair. "Girl, get out of the man's fridge. That's none of your business."

Tracey moved into the kitchen, running her hand along the new quartz countertop that he and Kenny had added.

"Very nice!" she said. "How long have you been working on it?"

"Since I moved back, on and off. But I've been more focused the last few months. The kitchen and living room have been the main projects. I'm looking to tackle some rooms upstairs next."

"My aunt would be impressed," Tracey said. "She's always saying old houses need to breathe and have their character respected even while updating them."

"That's exactly what I've been trying to do."

Their eyes met, and something passed between them. Tracey looked away first, turning her attention back to the exposed beam.

"This place feels peaceful," she said.

Emmett smiled. Some nights it did. One day, he hoped to completely feel the peace he desired. Some parts of the past still lingered. Memories of his dad drinking, his mother's scared voice and him keeping his younger siblings away from his parents' loud arguments.

And there was his occasional stalker.

From the kitchen, Kenny's voice carried to them. "Hey, Redd, where'd you put that pizza menu? You should at least feed your company."

Charlene called back. "I could eat. What about you, Tracey?"

Emmett caught Tracey's eyes again, her smile almost shy now. "Sure."

"Top drawer by the fridge," Emmett answered.

Thirty minutes into a steady stream of back and forth sibling banter between Kenny and Charlene, the pizza arrived. To Emmett, Tracey seemed more relaxed than he'd ever seen her. And for the first time, Emmett was really enjoying his home. He'd imagined a home filled with friends and food.

And maybe something else, as he snatched glances at Tracey, enjoying seeing her laugh.

The shrill ring of his phone cut through the moment. When he glanced at the screen, his good vibes vanished. While he'd been expecting this call, he wished it had come later after everyone left. He was having a good time and had briefly forgotten about the Whitaker murder investigation.

"Sorry, I need to take this." He stepped into the kitchen and then outside the back door, leaving it open a crack. Taking a breath, he answered the phone. "Hey, Jack. What's up?"

Jack's gruff voice came through the line. "I've been tracking the Whitakers like you asked. Helen barely leaves that house of hers. It's a wonder she drove the other day to see Darrell's daughter. Anyway, the daughter Rachel visits her almost daily, sometimes bringing groceries, that sort of thing."

"And Alex?" Emmett prompted.

"That's where it gets interesting. Man's busy, that's for sure. Council meetings, networking with clients, country club lunches, he's a regular ole' politician. But this afternoon, he made a visit outside of the county."

Emmett felt his pulse quicken. "Where?"

"Alex met up with Preston Langley."

Even though he was outside, Emmett lowered his voice. "You're certain it was Langley with Alex?"

"Yep, and Alex seemed very agitated. Not Langley though. That's one cool cucumber."

Emmett knew that from personal experience. Nothing seemed to faze that man. He was a bit too cold. "Where did they meet?"

"Langley's got a private dock on his property. Alex pulled up in his car, met Langley on the dock. They walked around the grounds. Couldn't get close enough to hear anything, but the body language tells a story. Alex waved his arms around, and Langley just stood there with his hands in his pockets. Then they disappeared into Langley's boathouse for about twenty minutes."

"Keep tracking him," Emmett said, his mind racing. "I think maybe it's time for me to ask Langley some questions directly." He turned, sensing he wasn't alone, and found Tracey standing in the doorway.

Jack said. "I got photos for you. I'll send them later."

He made eye contact with Tracey. "Thanks, Jack. I will be on the lookout for the photos."

"Langley? Preston Langley?" Her eyes narrowed. "The man you defended in that murder trial last year. Why do you need to talk to him?"

Emmett felt the floor drop out from under him. He didn't want to share this with her. "Tracey, that was a private conversation."

Her voice rose. "I wasn't eavesdropping. I just came to the door to see what happened to you." She stepped closer to him. "The man you helped walk free after he murdered his business partner? Should you be still doing work for him? I don't want anything to blow back on my father?"

That stung, especially coming from Tracey.

He stepped toward her. "My private detective has been tracking some new developments. I can't get into this with you right now. I'm digging in some tricky areas and I need proof."

She frowned. "What kind of proof? I have a right to know."

He rolled his shoulders, feeling the usual tension creep back in. "I'm looking more into the company that caused the Whitaker Construction Company's bankruptcy."

Kenny peered outside. "Everything okay out here?"

"Yeah," Emmett turned around. It unnerved him that they were talking out in the open. "We should go inside."

They all clambered back inside to his dining room table.

"What's going on?" Charlene moved to Tracey's side.

"Nothing. I'm following up on leads that Mr. Mac left me." Emmett took a deep breath, and looked directly at Tracey. "I need you to trust me."

Tracey looked away, crossing her arms like she was cold.

Charlene glanced at Tracey, before turning her attention to Emmett. "Do you think Dad was really close to something?"

"I do."

Tracey looked at Emmett. "I hope one of those leads is looking at the Whitakers."

He nodded. "When you told me Helen came to see you, I moved the family up on my list."

"Wait, what?" Kenny and Charlene said at the same time.

Tracey explained, "Helen just showed up at Sweetgrass."

Emmett added. "I heard she was a recluse, and the way Tracey explained the family's behavior, I felt like we needed to keep tabs on the Whitakers."

Tracey's eyes never left his face. "Do you know who killed James Whitaker? Who set my father up?"

The room fell silent as they all waited for his answer.

"Not yet," Emmett said carefully. "But I'm getting close."

Chapter 22

Tracey enjoyed the camaraderie with Emmett and the McMillan siblings. Kenny launched into him and his wife's desire for their third child to be a little girl. The conversation made her feel emotional. She always wondered if she could give Jayden a sibling. It had been lonely growing up as an only child and she hadn't wanted that for her son. Of course for her to have more children that would require her being in a relationship that led to marriage. In the years since Jordan's death, she'd not dated so it all seemed like a fantasy.

When Tracey attempted to leave, saying that they needed to pick up Jayden, Charlene and her brother grinned. She raised an eyebrow at her friend. "What's going on?"

Charlene rubbed her arm. "Nothing. No worries. I checked on Jayden a while ago and he's having a good time. Why don't you let him spend the night? Your aunt was happy to bring him some of his stuff."

Tracey wasn't sure she liked her aunt and friend making a decision about her son for her. But the glint in Charlene's eye kept her from voicing her objection. Instead, she leaned in. "Charlene, what are you and Aunt Edna up to?"

Charlene smirked. "Just giving you a little nudge and some time for you. And..." She glanced over at Emmett.

Tracey widened her eyes and protested.

Kenny came around the corner with his booming voice. "Thanks, Tracey, for letting Jayden hang out with us tonight. We'll take good care of him. He's going to have a blast with my boys."

She smiled, but shot daggers at her friend. "I appreciate it, Kenny."

"No problem." He winked. "Besides, I'm sure you and Redd got plenty to talk about."

She turned to catch Emmett pushing his glasses up his nose. His wide-eyed expression said he wasn't sure what was happening either. That made her feel better.

Just like that, both McMillan siblings left, leaving her with Emmett.

"Well, it looks like it's just me and you. Are you okay sticking around for a while?"

"Sure, but I'm at your mercy for a ride home since my friend abandoned me."

He laughed. "That was definitely a well-planned escape."

"Let me help you clean up."

They worked together in a comforting quiet. She studied his work in the kitchen, thinking it rivaled some of the design work she admired on *HGTV*, one of her personal vices. Emmett had very sophisticated taste, which she liked. After they finished cleaning up, she joined him in his living room. They hadn't talked about the investigation, but it hung between them now that the cleaning was behind them.

Tracey sat next to him on the couch, wondering if maybe they were sitting too close to each other. She placed her hands in her lap, not sure what to do with them. "I want to help with the investigation," she said quietly. "My dad shouldn't have this lingering over him now."

Emmett turned his head and met her gaze. "I have plenty of help with this. You need to spend the time with your father. I promise you I will not rest until I clear your father's name."

The sound of tires on gravel outside broke the moment. Tracey thought the headlights were awfully bright. "I'm sure that's not Kenny or Charlene coming back. Maybe someone is turning around in your driveway."

"Maybe." Emmett frowned as he reached for his phone on the table.

The alarm in his eyes made Tracey's stomach flutter. "What's wrong?"

He jumped up from the couch. "I'm sorry! I have an unwanted visitor."

Tracey stood with him, crossing her arms around her midsection in a protective stance. She wanted to look out the window but noticed Emmett focused on his phone. Peering over his shoulder, she saw that he was looking at a live security camera feed. "Who is it? Is it Langley?"

He shook his head. "No, but the man is not a fan of Langley... or me. It's Arnold Sullivan."

"Sullivan?" Then it hit her. "He's related to Bobby Sullivan. And he's showing up at your house? You need to call the police."

"I've filed reports before. They can't do much unless he actually threatens me." Emmett walked over to the door. "I think I should talk to him. I've got to put a stop to this."

Tracey's voice rose. "Are you kidding? You can't go out there." She ran up behind him and grabbed his upper arm, where the muscle was hard and tense.

"I'll handle it," Emmett squared his shoulders. He turned as if he was going to head up the stairs, but looked at her instead. He placed his hands on her shoulders. "You stay inside."

She shook her head. "This isn't right. I'm calling the cops."

Emmett hesitated, then nodded. "You call. I'll try to keep him talking until they arrive."

"Emmett," Tracey grabbed his arm again, "be careful."

She frantically dialed while trying to keep her eyes on Emmett as he opened his door. All she could see was a large figure approaching the porch.

"Sullivan," Emmett called out. "This is private property. You need to leave."

The voice that answered back slurred as if the man had been drinking. "You think I haven't noticed? First, Langley, now Boyd? You make a habit of freeing murderers?"

Tracey heard Emmett's answer. "Darrell Boyd was wrongfully convicted. And he's dying of cancer. All I'm trying to do is get him proper medical care."

Sullivan gave a harsh laugh. "Whatever you say. Another killer walks free." He took a step forward. "My brother's children still cry for their daddy. His wife still sleeps alone. And Preston Langley is walking around in this world as if he did nothing."

"I understand you're hurting—"

"You understand nothing!" Sullivan roared, surging forward. "You're just as guilty as Langley! You knew what he did, and you got him off anyway."

Fear crawled up Tracey's spine. The dispatcher promised the police would be there soon. But would they be here on time? She stepped up further, hoping if the man saw her, he might leave Emmett alone.

As if sensing her behind him, Emmett glanced over his shoulder and held up his arm, wanting her to stay back.

"The law isn't always just, Sullivan. Nobody knows that better than me." Emmett took a deep breath. "Harassing me won't bring your brother back."

Sullivan's face contorted. "No, but it might stop you from freeing another murderer." He reached behind his back. When his hand emerged, he was holding something.

Tracey screamed. "Emmett."

"Sullivan, put that gun down." Emmett backed up a step. "You don't want to do this."

"Actually, I do," Sullivan growled, taking another step up. "You ruined my family's chance for justice. An eye for an eye, Counselor."

Tracey yelled. "The police are on their way."

Sullivan's gaze shifted to Tracey. "Who the hell are you?"

"I'm Darrell Boyd's daughter," she walked up behind Emmett. He held out his arm placing his body in front of hers. "My father is innocent, and you will not mess up his chance to be free."

Sullivan hesitated. "Your father killed his business partner."

"No," Tracey shouted. "He was framed. And we're going to prove it. So you need to ask yourself, do you really want to go to prison for assaulting a lawyer who's trying to free an innocent man?"

In the distance, sirens wailed. Sullivan's eyes darted from Tracey to Emmett to the road. He backed down the steps, pointing the barrel of the gun at Emmett. "I'm watching you, Craig." Sullivan retreated to his truck just as the police cruiser turned into the driveway, lights flashing.

Tracey held her hands to her face. "Thank you, Lord."

They watched as the officers approached Sullivan's truck, one hand on their holsters. It took some time, but they took Arnold away in handcuffs.

Tracey wrapped her hand around Emmett's arm. "Maybe this will keep him away."

He didn't appear to hear her, but she felt his arm stiffen. She pulled away, feeling the warmth that had existed between them earlier evaporate.

"I'll get you home as soon as we finish giving our statements," he said. "I'm sorry about all of this, Tracey."

"It's fine. Things could have been worse."

"That's exactly what I was worried about," he muttered, more to himself than to her. "My past mistakes. They shouldn't become your problem."

"Emmett—"

"You'll be heading back to Florida soon anyway," he continued, avoiding her gaze. "And that's probably for the best."

The words stung more than Tracey expected. She'd been so caught up in their growing connection tonight, she'd almost forgotten she was only here for another week.

"Right."

An officer approached, notebook in hand.

Despite the adrenaline from the situation, Tracey felt like a special opportunity had been lost.

Chapter 23

Beaufort Memorial Hospital
Sunday, May 25 at 10:23 a.m. EST

Though she tried to hide it, the events of last night had left Tracey rattled. Sullivan's rage-contorted face kept flashing in her mind. If the police hadn't arrived when they did... And Emmett. He was so quiet when he dropped her off last night. She could tell he was kicking himself from what happened. But it wasn't his fault.

"Mom? Are you okay?"

She looked down to find Jayden studying her with concern beyond his years.

"I'm fine, sweetie. You ready to meet your grandpa?"

Aunt Edna stood beside them in her Sunday best, a royal blue dress with matching hat. "Darrell's going to be over the moon to see how big you've gotten."

Jayden skipped down the corridor between them, his hand in Tracey's, asking questions about everything he saw. "Will Grandpa have tubes and machines like on TV?"

"Some," Tracey answered honestly. "But they're just to help him feel better."

"Because he's really sick?"

"Yes, baby."

They reached the security checkpoint where a corrections officer sat outside her father's room. The man's presence was a stark reminder that despite the medical transfer, her father was still technically a prisoner.

The officer checked their IDs against his clipboard. "You have one hour," he told them. "I'll be right here the whole time."

When they entered the room, her father sat propped up against pillows. His eyes lit up when he saw them, and when his gaze fell on Jayden, they filled with tears. Tracey's heart clenched at the sight.

"Hello, Daddy," Tracey moved to his bedside with Jayden trailing behind her.

"My baby girl." His voice was a rasp. Then he looked past her to Jayden, who peeked from behind Tracey. "And this must be my grandson."

Jayden stepped forward cautiously. "Hi, Grandpa."

A smile transformed Darrell's gaunt face. "Come closer, young man. Let me get a good look at you."

With gentle encouragement from Tracey, Jayden approached the bed. Darrell reached out a trembling hand, which Jayden took without hesitation.

"You look just like your daddy," Darrell said, his voice thick with emotion. "Same eyes. Same smile."

"That's what Grandma Lydia says too," Jayden replied.

A shadow crossed Darrell's face at the mention of Lydia, but he recovered quickly. "Well, she's right about that. Your daddy was a fine basketball player, you know. Best in the county."

"I know! I saw his trophies. And I made three baskets in a row on his old hoop!"

Edna moved to the other side of the bed, bending to kiss her brother's cheek. "You're looking better today. The color's coming back to your face."

"Always the optimist, sis," Darrell chuckled.

While Jayden showed his grandfather drawings he'd made and told him about school in Florida, Tracey watched the scene with a lump in her throat. This was how it should have been all along. Her son growing up knowing his grandfather. Five years of birthdays, holidays, and so much more had been lost and could never be recovered.

When Jayden grew restless, Edna suggested they go find a snack in the cafeteria. "Your mama needs some time alone with your grandpa," she said, taking Jayden's hand. "We'll get some ice cream."

After Edna and Jayden left, Tracey moved closer to her father's bed, taking his hand in hers. "How are you really feeling, Dad?"

"I've had better days," he admitted. "But seeing Jayden has given me more strength than any medicine could."

"He's been so excited to see you. Hasn't stopped talking about it since we planned this visit."

A comfortable silence fell between them. Tracey thought about everything that had happened in the past week. Helen's strange visit to Sweetgrass, Alex and Rachel's strange behavior, Langley, Arnold Sullivan and Emmett.

She couldn't stop thinking about Emmett. She knew he was working on trying to find James's killer. But he was facing his own danger.

"Dad," she began hesitantly. "Did Aunt Edna tell you about our surprise visitor last week?"

He listened intently as Tracey recounted Helen's unexpected visit to the bed-and-breakfast, her confused state, Alex's angry reaction and Rachel's apology.

Her father's brow furrowed. "I can't believe Helen came to see you after all these years?"

"She seemed troubled, Dad. Like she wanted to tell us something but couldn't get the words out." Tracey fiddled with her fingernails. "Then when Alex showed up, it was like she just shut down."

Darrell was quiet for a long moment, staring at the ceiling. "Helen and James. Their marriage wasn't what people thought."

"Yeah, Helen said something similar when she came to Sweetgrass, but what does that mean?"

"James could be a hard man to live with. Charming in public, different behind closed doors." He coughed, wincing with the effort. "Especially toward the end."

Tracey leaned forward. "The end? Before he was killed?"

"Things changed when Alex started working at the company. James was hard on him. I'd asked him one time why he pushed the boy and criticized him like he did. He told me to mind my business. I felt kind of bad for the young man. Nothing Alex did was ever good enough for James." Darrell's eyes grew distant. "I saw them arguing more than once. Helen would call the office, frantic, asking if Alex was there."

"Sounds like James was abusive, in a way. Funny, I never took him as that kind of person."

Her father shifted uncomfortably. "Your mama and Edna used to tell me to watch my back around James. I can't tell you why I trusted that man so much. Sure, we were good friends when we were younger, but I saw the worst of him."

Tracey's mind raced. "Do you think the Whitakers could have turned on each other? Could Alex have—?"

"I don't know," Darrell cut her off. "I just know I didn't kill James."

"Emmett thinks Preston Langley is connected somehow. That he had business dealings with the Whitakers. Do you remember him?"

Darrell took a deep breath. The effort caused him to cough.

Tracey jumped from her seat. "Are you okay? Should we call a nurse?"

He waved at her to sit back down. "I'm fine. You're talking about the guy involved in the resort project. Coastal Developments. It came out of nowhere, promising big money. James was excited at first, then something changed. He became secretive, shutting me out of meetings."

"Meetings with Langley?"

"I never met him. James would just say I needed to keep my eye on operations." Darrell's face appeared sad, then angry. "But Alex was always included."

Tracey frowned, not realizing how much she hadn't understood about her father's relationship with his supposed partner. "That doesn't seem fair to leave you out like that. You might have talked some sense into them."

Her father grinned. "That could have been true. At first, I wasn't sure why. Then, I realized James must have been wanting to prepare the boy for taking on the business. Which is another reason I couldn't understand why he wanted to file for bankruptcy if he was investing time in that boy to take on the business."

Before Tracey could press further, the door opened and Jayden bounded in.

"Grandpa, they had chocolate and vanilla and strawberry! Aunt E let me get the biggest ice cream cone!"

The serious conversation ended as Jayden chattered excitedly about the cafeteria. Before they knew it, the officer knocked on the door, signaling their time was up. Tracey looked at her phone, noticing the officer let them stay long past the allotted hour.

Jayden hugged his grandfather goodbye, promising to draw him more pictures. Edna kissed her brother's forehead, whispering something in his ear that made him smile.

When it was Tracey's turn, she leaned close, not wanting Jayden to hear. "I'm going to clear your name, Dad. I promise."

"Be careful, baby girl," he whispered back. "Whoever framed me has gotten away with murder for seven years. They won't want the truth coming out now."

With Jayden skipping ahead in front of them, Tracey and Edna walked back through the hospital corridor.

Tracey knew Emmett wouldn't want her to get involved, but she had to know, not only for her father's sake, but hers too. By the time they reached the parking lot, a plan emerged in her mind.

Tracey pulled out her phone and typed a quick message to Emmett.

I'm going to talk to Helen.

Chapter 24

Emmett continued to struggle with the image of Sullivan's face at his doorstep last night. What bothered him more was Tracey being caught in the middle. Thanks to Charlene and Kenny, they'd had a great time. And then Sullivan showed up, destroying what was building between them.

Emmett pulled his BWM into the empty lot of a closed roadside fruit stand about a half-mile from his real destination. Jack Daniels's weathered pickup truck was already parked in the shade of a large oak tree. Emmett climbed out of his car and approached the pickup, where Jack sat with a pair of binoculars in his lap and a thermos of coffee in hand.

Jack observed Emmett as he slid onto the passenger seat. "You sure you up to this, Counselor?"

"Didn't get much sleep," Emmett admitted. "Sullivan showed up at my house last night."

Jack's eyebrows shot up. "Bobby Sullivan's brother? What happened?"

"The cops took him away." Emmett confirmed. "Tracey was there. She heard what he said about her father."

Jack whistled low. "That could've gotten ugly."

"It almost did. If the police hadn't shown up when they did..." Emmett trailed off, not wanting to consider what might have happened. "You got anything for me before I go in here to see Langley."

Jack reached behind his seat and pulled out a manila folder. "I've been digging through old records. Take a look."

Emmett opened the folder to find photocopied yearbook photos. The first showed a young Helen Whitaker, then Helen Barnes, according to the caption. Her blonde hair feathered in the style of the era, smiling next to a handsome, dark-haired young man.

"Is that Langley?" Emmett asked, though he already knew the answer. The younger man's face held the same sharp features and confident gaze.

"They were quite the item," Jack confirmed. "Homecoming king and queen."

Emmett flipped through more photos of Helen and Preston at various Charleston High School events, always together. "What happened?"

"From what I could piece together, Langley left for college up north after graduation. Helen stayed in Charleston. Met James Whitaker, eldest son of one of Beaufort's most prominent families, and they married after college."

Emmett stared at the clipping, the implication clear. "You think Helen might have rekindled her love for Langley or Langley reached out to Helen?"

Jack said, "That would explain a lot. Like why Langley suddenly took an interest in Whitaker Construction. Maybe he was interested in getting closer to a past love."

Emmett closed the folder, his mind racing. "This is all interesting, but there's no way to put Langley near James when he was murdered. Was he in town?"

"Unfortunately, no. But I thought this might give some new insight into the Whitakers."

Emmett sighed. "I will ask him about Helen and Alex. Maybe he will reveal something."

Jack reached into his jacket pocket. "At least wear this." He held out what looked like a pen. "Audio recorder. It won't hold up in court, but it might give us something to work with."

Emmett hesitated, then took the device. "You'll be nearby?"

"I'll be watching the entrance to Preston Heights," Jack confirmed. "Any sign of trouble, I'm calling in every favor I've got with the department."

"Appreciate that," Emmett said getting out of Jack's truck. With a resolved sigh, he climbed back into his car and headed toward Langley's house.

Sunday, May 24 at 2:05 p.m. EST

The security guard at the entrance didn't even blink when Emmett gave his name. "Mr. Langley mentioned you might stop by, Mr. Craig. Go right ahead."

That stopped Emmett cold. Langley was expecting him? He hadn't called ahead, hadn't told anyone where he was going after meeting with Jack. Yet somehow Langley knew he was coming.

Emmett's stomach tightened as he drove along the winding driveway. He remembered the first time he'd arrived at the impressive house out in the country. With this being his first big case back in Beaufort, he believed in the charms of Preston Langley. Believed the businessman had been wrongfully accused. How wrong Emmett had been about that!

Langley's house was almost too modern against the large oak trees. Emmett could see the water beyond the house where expensive boats were docked. In the front of the house, a black Escalade was parked beside a sleek red sports car.

Emmett had barely stepped from his car when the front door opened. Langley emerged with a crystal tumbler in his hand. "Counselor," his voice carried across the manicured lawn. "I was wondering when I would see you again."

"We need to talk," Emmett said, stopping at the foot of the steps leading to the front door.

Langley's smile didn't reach his eyes. "Always so direct. I appreciated that about you in court." He gestured with his glass. "Come in. I'm having a scotch."

Emmett followed Langley into the house. The interior was just as he remembered. Expensive and cold, despite the designer furniture and extensive artwork. This was a house meant to impress, not to be lived in.

He followed Langley into an open living area. Langley settled into a leather armchair, gesturing for Emmett to sit opposite him. "What can I do for you? Or rather, what questions can I answer about Whitaker?"

Emmett remained standing. "How did you know I was here to ask about Whitaker?"

Langley's laugh was soft and without humor. "The moment I heard you took on Boyd's case, I expected you. I know how you work. And Mr. McMillan also had questions. You took on this case from him, correct? He was a mentor of yours?"

Emmett hadn't considered that Mr. Mac had reached out to Langley. Maybe that's why Mr. Mac was so against him taking on Langley as a client.

"I understand you brought James Whitaker a resort proposition. You worked with Whitaker and his son Alex."

There was a brief flicker across Langley's features. He took another sip from his tumbler.

"The resort project was one of my less successful ventures. We lost several key investors right before breaking ground." He looked up, meeting Emmett's gaze. "I actually felt bad about how things went with James. He'd invested considerable resources into the preparations."

"You felt bad for James," Emmett repeated. "What about Helen? Did you feel bad for her too?"

Langley's hand stilled on his glass. "Helen? What does she have to do with a failed business venture?"

Emmett said. "You and Helen were together long before she married James."

Langley didn't deny it. Instead, a subtle smile played at his lips. "Ancient history, Counselor. People have pasts."

"Is it history?" Emmett pressed. "You still see the Whitakers, don't you? You're still part of their lives?"

"What exactly are you getting at?" Langley's voice took on an edge.

"Alex Whitaker." Emmett watched Langley's face carefully. "He still meets with you regularly. Even after your project bankrupted the family company."

Langley's expression hardened. "Alex has proven himself quite capable in the years since his father's unfortunate death."

Emmett paused, trying to keep up with his racing thoughts while squeezing what he could from Langley. "I'm curious. Did Alex's relationship with his father break down because of the resort proposition? Did James blame his son when things went south?"

Langley set his glass on the coffee table. "Why are you throwing out these theories, Counselor? What do you hope to gain here?"

Emmett took in a breath. "You spent a lot of time with James and Alex. You had to have seen how desperate Alex was to prove himself to his father. He brought you into the company, vouched for the resort project. Do you think James would have taken it out on his son?"

"James Whitaker had a temper," Langley admitted. "Brilliant businessman, but not always the most understanding father." His eyes took on a distant quality. "Alex deserved better."

Puzzled, Emmett caught a subtle shift in Langley's demeanor. Then something came to him the more he stared at Langley.

Why hadn't he seen this before?

Langley's gaze snapped back to Emmett. "You know, you're a fine lawyer, Craig. You notice things others miss." He stood, moving to the bar to refill his glass. "What would you really like to know, Counselor? What are you fishing for?"

"You should know I am seeking the truth about what happened to James Whitaker," Emmett replied. "Tell me about your continued friendship with Alex. Are you like his mentor now?"

A smile spread across Langley's face. "Let's just say I've taken an interest in the young man's career." His voice dropped slightly. "He has... potential. Reminds me of myself at that age."

"I bet he does," Emmett said quietly. "Almost like father and son."

The temperature in the room seemed to drop ten degrees. Langley's expression hardened, his easy manner vanishing.

"You're not just Alex's mentor," Emmett pressed. "You're his biological father."

Langley stated flatly. "You're a clever man, Craig."

"Did James find out? Is that why he was killed?"

Langley's eyes flashed. "I had nothing to do with James Whitaker's death. That's the truth, whether you believe it or not."

"And Alex? What about him?"

"You know," Langley said. "You're still bound by our confidential relationship, even though the case is closed."

"This isn't about my career," Emmett replied. "It's about a man dying in prison for a crime he didn't commit."

"How noble," Langley mocked. "The crusading attorney determined to right wrongs. But we both know better, don't we? This is about your guilt." He moved closer, his voice dropping. "And maybe about the lovely Ms. Boyd? I hear you've been spending a considerable amount of time together."

The mention of Tracey sent ice through Emmett's veins. It wasn't a casual remark.

Emmett asked. "Are you spying on me?"

Something dangerous flashed in Langley's eyes. "Stay away from Alex," he warned, all pretense of civility vanishing. "You're barking up the wrong tree."

"I don't think I am," Emmett countered. He could tell he was getting closer to the truth. "I think Alex was there the night James died. I think there was an argument—son against father. Things got heated. Maybe a paperweight was grabbed in anger."

"You're treading on very thin ice," Langley's voice dropped to a near whisper.

"You might be able to get away with your crimes, Langley," Emmett said, holding his ground. "But your son? He's already unraveling."

Langley set his glass down with enough force that amber liquid sloshed over the rim. "This conversation is over." Langley moved toward the door, a clear dismissal. "There's nothing connecting me to James Whitaker's death. Nothing connecting Alex either. Just speculation from a lawyer desperate to redeem himself."

Emmett left, unhappy about Langley keeping tabs on him and his work with Boyd. He especially didn't like that Langley knew about Tracey.

Back in his car, Emmett called Jack. "Did you get all that on this audio device of yours?"

"Every single word. How did you guess Alex was his son?"

"It's all in the eyes. The way they talk. Not sure how I hadn't noticed before."

Jack whistled. "Be sure you watch your back. It's one thing to have Langley as your enemy, but what if he warns Alex that you're on to him?"

"Yeah, I know. We need to look back at where Alex was that night. Also, check on the whereabouts of the other Whitakers while we're at it."

"I'm on it."

After hanging up with Jack, Emmett looked down at his phone. He'd received a message from Tracey.

I'm going to talk to Helen.

"No, no. Tracey, what are you doing?"

Emmett took off from Langley's house. "Hey, Siri. Call Edna Boyd." Technology was a wonder for handsfree phone calls.

"Emmett? Good to hear from you."

"Hello, Edna. Is Tracey there?"

Edna answered, "No, she dropped me and Jayden off at the house. Said she had somewhere to go. Is everything okay?"

He gripped the steering wheel. "Yes. Hey, Edna, can you text me the Whitaker's address?"

"Any reason why?"

Emmett gritted his teeth. "I want to see if I can catch Alex, that's all."

He waited for Edna to send the text, but before he could see it, his phone rang.

"Tracey. Where are you?"

Emmett could hear voices in the background. He pressed the accelerator.

Chapter 25

Beaufort, South Carolina
Sunday, May 24 at 2:00 p.m. EST

Tracey made some excuse to her aunt, trying not to tell her where she was actually going. She knew Aunt Edna would talk her out of what she was about to do.

The Whitaker home stood at the end of a tree-lined drive in Beaufort's historic district, a sprawling antebellum masterpiece with white columns and wraparound porches. Tracey had been here frequently as a child, but not since her mother's death. The house had seemed magical then.

She parked her car on the street rather than in the circular driveway, half-expecting to be turned away before she even reached the door. She had no idea if Rachel or Alex were there.

A housekeeper answered her knock. "Can I help you, Miss?"

"I'd like to speak with Mrs. Whitaker," Tracey said.

"Mrs. Whitaker isn't receiving visitors today," the housekeeper's eyes darted behind her into the interior of the house.

"Alice? Who is it?" Helen's voice called from somewhere inside.

"Tell her it's Tracey Boyd."

With a slight nod, Alice stepped back and let Tracey inside.

"Wait here." As soon as the housekeeper disappeared into the house, Tracey pulled her phone out. Now that she was here, she felt foolish for coming. If anyone needed to be aware of what was going on, it would be Emmett. She pressed his number and slipped her phone back into her bag, hearing the housekeeper approach.

Tracey looked up at the wide staircase that curved up into the second story. Family photos of James and Helen on their wedding day, Alex and Rachel in graduation caps, grandchildren in Easter clothes. A family's history had been carefully curated up the wall of the staircase.

The housekeeper stood in front of her. "Mrs. Whitaker will see you now."

She led Tracey to a sitting room, where Helen sat on a small loveseat. Her silver-blonde hair had been swept into a loose bun, but sprigs of hair framed her face.

"Tracey." Her voice was warm. "It's so good to see you."

"Hello, Miss Helen. I won't take much of your time."

Helen smiled. "Dear, you can take much time as you need." She held her hand over her heart. "You look so much like Judith."

Tracey settled into an armchair across from Helen, noticing how the older woman's hands trembled slightly as she adjusted a shawl around her shoulders.

"You came to Sweetgrass the other day," Tracey began. "You seemed to have something important to tell me."

Helen's eyes clouded. "Did I? I'm afraid my memory isn't what it used to be."

"You said you should have spoken up," Tracey pressed. "That you felt guilty about my father being in prison. What did you mean, Miss Helen?"

The older woman's gaze drifted to the window. "Your mother was my dearest friend. When she got sick, I promised her I'd look out for you." Her voice broke. "I didn't keep that promise very well."

"My father is dying," Tracey said quietly. "If you know something that could help clear his name—"

"It was a terrible night," Helen interrupted suddenly. "James came home in such a state. I'd never seen him so angry."

Tracey leaned forward. "The night he died?"

Helen shook her head. "The night before. He'd found out something that devastated him." She wrung her hands. "He confronted me with it. Called me terrible names. Said I'd made a fool of him for decades."

"What did he find out?"

Helen's eyes met Tracey's, tears threatening to fall. "That Alex wasn't his son."

Tracey sucked in a breath. That was the last thing she'd expected Helen to say.

"All those years," Helen continued, her voice stronger now. "I'd kept the secret. But somehow, James discovered the truth. He threatened to disown Alex, to tell everyone in Beaufort about my indiscretion."

Who was his father? Tracey thought. But she asked. "What happened? Did James and Alex have a fight?"

Helen shook her head. "Alex didn't know. I still wasn't sure how James found out. Preston said he never breathed a word. James was so upset that he didn't come home the next night. Said he would spend the night in his office. So I went to see him. But he wouldn't listen. He wouldn't listen."

Tracey's heart lurched at what she was hearing.

Preston? Preston Langley.

"Mother, what are you doing?"

Tracey turned to see Alex standing there, his face tight. Behind him, Rachel hovered.

Tracey sat up straighter, hoping the connection on her phone had reached Emmett. Had he heard anything that Helen said?

"Alex, I didn't know you were home," Helen said, shrinking back in her chair.

"Clearly." His cold gaze fixed on Tracey. "Tracey was just leaving."

"Tracey just arrived." Helen huffed.

Alex strode into the room, positioning himself between Tracey and his mother. "Mother isn't well," he said to Tracey. "She gets confused, says things that don't make sense."

"I'm not confused today, Alex." Helen's gaze never wavered from her son's face. "I haven't taken those pills you and Dr. Meyers insist I need." She turned to Tracey. "They don't want me to remember what happened that night. What I did."

Alex's face hardened. "That's enough."

"Tracey deserves the truth." Helen's eyes filled with tears. "Judith was my dearest friend, and I've let her daughter suffer while her father sat in prison for something he didn't do. Poor Darrell. He was so loyal to James."

Rachel whined. "Think about what you're saying, Mother."

The room fell silent as Helen stared at her children. Then she looked back at Tracey.

"I went to James's office that night," Helen said, her voice calm. "I begged him not to disown Alex. We argued. There was that paperweight on his desk..." Her voice faltered.

"Mother, stop this!" Alex stepped toward her, but Helen held up her hand.

"I didn't mean to hit him so hard," her voice strained. "I just wanted him to stop shouting, to listen to me. But he fell, and there was so much blood..."

Tracey's heart hammered in her chest as the implications of Helen's confession washed over her.

"You killed him," Tracey snapped. "And then you let my father take the blame."

"I didn't want my Alex ruined. My poor boy didn't deserve that."

Alex's face went deathly pale at his mother's confession.

Rachel gasped, her hand covering her mouth. "Mother, what are you saying?"

Helen nodded slowly. "I never told anyone. Not even you, Alex." Her eyes filled with regret. "It was before I married your father. Preston discovered you were his son years ago." She frowned. "He approached you, didn't he?"

Alex shook his head in disbelief. "What? He just wanted to invest in the company. Said he saw potential in me." He stumbled backward until he found the edge of a chair to steady himself.

Helen said softly. "I wish I'd known he'd reached out to you. Preston was always a hard man. I blamed myself for not being honest with him and James. I might have saved everyone from the heartache and repercussions of Preston's choices."

Tracey could hardly believe what she was hearing.

Rachel's shoulders slumped as she crossed to her mother's side. "I came home that night. Found Mother cleaning up blood from her clothes." Her voice shook. "She told me what happened, that it was an accident."

"And you helped cover it up," Tracey said. "By planting the evidence in my father's truck? Framing my father for something he didn't do and then blackballing him in this small town, ensuring his guilt before a trial ever commenced."

Rachel protested weakly. "What was I supposed to do? Turn our own mother in?"

"But you let my father go to prison!" Tracey's voice rose with anger.

Alex seemed to recover slightly from the shock of learning about his parentage. He looked at his sister and then his mother, his eyes wide. "The police focused on Darrell because of the argument. All the evidence pointed to him."

"Because you made it happen that way!" Tracey shouted.

The doorbell rang incessantly, making all of them go silent.

Alex jumped up. "Who can that be? Tracey, what have you done?"

Tracey stood and stepped back. "What have I done? This is all on y'all. You did this."

"Stop it! All of you. Please!" Helen stood, flinging her arms out as if to keep her son away from Tracey.

"Tracey?"

Tracey turned to the doorway at the sound of her name. Emmett walked into the room and straight toward her. "Are you okay?"

Her body shook from the revelations the Whitakers laid on her. She was so relieved to see Emmett. Words wouldn't come to her, but he seemed to know. He placed an arm around her shoulders.

Emmett turned to the Whitakers. "Detective Simmons will pay you all a visit. Mrs. Whitaker, I'm Emmett Craig, Darrell Boyd's lawyer."

Helen dropped her arms at her side, suddenly looking very exhausted. "It's good to meet you, Mr. Craig. We must make sure Tracey gets to spend time with Darrell."

As Emmett promised, Detective Simmons arrived. Tracey went outside to the garden, Emmett beside her.

"Did you hear everything on the phone?"

He stepped up and placed his arm on her shoulder. "I did. I'm glad you called me."

She leaned into him, feeling jittery. "I had to do something. I just wanted to know what Helen was trying to tell us. I didn't know it would be all of that."

When his strong arms came around her, she cried.

Epilogue

Beaufort, South Carolina
Friday, July 4 at 7:38 p.m. EST

An occasional breeze drifted off the water as Darrell Boyd sat on the Sweetgrass porch in one of the blue rocking chairs. He grinned as his grandson chased fireflies across the lawn.

"Got another one!" Jayden called out, cupping his hands around the glowing insect before rushing up the porch steps to show his grandfather. "See how bright it is?"

Darrell leaned forward, his movements slow but steady. Six weeks of proper medical care had made a difference, though everyone understood care was not a cure. It was only buying time. "When I was your age, I used to catch them in jars."

"Mom says we shouldn't do that because they need to be free," Jayden replied, opening his hands to let the firefly escape.

"Your mama's a smart woman."

Jayden flopped onto the porch swing. "You didn't always listen to your mama when you were a kid. Aunt E told me about the time you jumped off the dock even though your mom said not to."

Darrell chuckled. "Your Aunt Edna talks too much." He glanced toward the door. "Speaking of your mama, she's been getting ready for quite a while now."

"That's because she likes Mr. Emmett," Jayden said. "She always takes forever when we're going to see him."

Darrell raised an eyebrow. "Is that so?"

Jayden nodded solemnly. "She smiles differently around him. And she lets him help with stuff, even though she usually does everything herself."

Darrell murmured. "You notice a lot."

A car turned into the driveway, pulling Jayden's attention away. "He's here!" The boy leaped off the swing and bounded down the steps as Emmett's BMW came to a stop.

Emmett stepped out of the car wearing khaki shorts and a light blue polo shirt. He waved to Darrell as Jayden skipped beside him.

"Will they be super loud? Do they let you get close enough to see the people lighting them? Can we get cotton candy?"

Emmett laughed, ruffling Jayden's hair. "Slow down, buddy. One question at a time." He climbed the porch steps, hand extended toward Darrell. "Evening, Darrell. How are you feeling today?"

"Can't complain," Darrell shook Emmett's hand. "Dr. Patel tells me I'm doing better than expected."

"That's good to hear."

The screen door opened, and both men turned as Tracey stepped onto the porch. She wore a simple sundress, white with tiny red and blue stars, her hair gathered in a loose bun with a few curls framing her face.

Emmett's expression softened in a way that wasn't lost on Darrell.

"Sorry to keep everyone waiting," Tracey said, her eyes meeting Emmett's briefly before darting away.

"Worth the wait," Emmett cleared his throat. "But we should get going if we want a good spot. The waterfront will be packed."

Jayden tugged at his mother's hand. "Can we get ice cream before the fireworks?"

"We'll see." Tracey bent to kiss her father's cheek. "Are you sure you don't want to come?"

Darrell patted her hand. "I'm sure. I can see the fireworks just fine from right here. Besides, you know my sister likes to keep me close."

Jayden hugged his grandfather, careful of the IV port still attached to his arm. "I'll tell you which ones were the best. The big boom ones or the sparkly ones."

"You do that," Darrell laughed. "Have fun."

Tracey lingered as Emmett led Jayden toward the car. "The medication is on the side table. Two pills if the pain gets bad."

"Tracey," her father interrupted gently. "I'll be fine. Go enjoy yourself."

She nodded, her expression caught between joy and sadness.

Emmett called from the driveway. "We'd better hurry if we want that ice cream before the show starts!"

As Tracey headed to the car, Darrell smiled.

Judith, I think our little girl will be happy, and I will be happy to see you soon.

Emmett found a parking spot remarkably close to the waterfront park. As they walked toward the gathering crowd, Jayden ran ahead, drawn by the carnival atmosphere of vendors and games set up for the celebration.

"Stay where we can see you," Tracey called after him.

"He'll be fine," Emmett assured her, his hand finding the small of her back, guiding her through the crowd.

They found a spot on the grassy area overlooking the river. Emmett spread out the blanket he'd brought while Tracey monitored Jayden, who was now captivated by a nearby face-painting booth.

"So, it's official?" Emmett asked as they settled onto the blanket.

"The Morrison," Tracey nodded. "Yes, I turned in my resignation and broke the lease on our apartment. I'll need to make another trip to sort out what I'm going to sell and what I will move here. I have some pieces that could fit nicely into the Sweetgrass."

Emmett's face broke into a wide smile. "I'm glad you and Jadyen will stay."

She bumped his arm with hers, returning a smile. "Aunt Edna needs help with Sweetgrass, especially now with Dad living downstairs again. I just need to register Jayden for school in the fall. He already has Kenny's boys as friends."

"I'm glad." Emmett brushed her hand before holding it.

Their eyes met, the moment stretching between them until Jayden came running back, his face now adorned with red and blue stars. "Can we get ice cream now? They have the kind with sprinkles!"

"Lead the way," Emmett said, standing and offering his hand to help Tracey up.

Following Jayden toward the ice cream vendor, Emmett's hand found hers again, and their fingers intertwined. It felt natural, as if they'd been doing this for years instead of weeks.

They grabbed their ice cream and returned back to the blanket just in time. Above them, the first firework shot into the sky, exploding in a shower of red and gold. Jayden jumped up and down in excitement. Tracey leaned against Emmett's chest, watching the colors reflect off the water.

It was good to be home!

About the Author

Tyora Moody is the author of **Soul-Searching Mysteries,** which includes **cozy mystery, women sleuth mystery,** and **romantic suspense** under the Christian Fiction genre. Her books include the Eugeena Patterson Mysteries, Joss Miller Mysteries, Serena Manchester Mysteries, Reed Family Mysteries, and the Victory Gospel Mysteries.

When Tyora isn't working for a literary client, she's either loving on her cats, listening to an audiobook or podcast, binge-watching crime shows or Marvel movies, and of course, thinking about the next book.

To contact Tyora about reviewing her books or book club discussions, visit her online at TyoraMoody.com.

Join her newsletter at https://tyoramoody.substack.com/

Tyora Moody's Books

Eugeena Patterson Mysteries
Deep Fried Trouble, #1
Oven Baked Secrets, #2
Lemon Filled Disaster, #3
A Simmering Dilemma, #4
An Unsavory Mess, #5
A Spicy Predicament, #6
Marinated Conditions, #7

Eugeena Patterson Family Shorts
Shattered Dreams, #1
A Blended Family Christmas, #2
Falling in Love... Again!, #3

Joss Miller Mysteries
Double Mocha Blues, #1
A Latte Mayhem, #2
Mint-Flavored Trouble, #3

Serena Manchester Mysteries
Hostile Eyewitness, prequel
Bittersweet Motives, #1
Dangerous Confessions, #2
Waning Innocence, #3
Presumed Guilty, #4
Shifting Blame, #5

Lowcountry Secrets (Romantic Suspense)
The Homecoming, #1

Reed Family Mysteries
Broken Heart, #1
Troubled Heart, #2
Relentless Heart, #3
With All My Heart, #3.5
Faithful Heart, #4
Wounded Heart, #5

Victory Gospel Series (Mysteries)
When Rain Falls, #1
When Memories Fade, #2
When Perfection Fails, #3

Victory Gospel Shorts (Sweet Romance)
The Replacement Date, #1

Southern Delights, #2
When Love Finds Me, #3
Nobody's Replacement, #4
A Southern Delights Christmas, #5
Holding on to Love, #6

www.ingramcontent.com/pod-product-compliance
Lightning Source LLC
Chambersburg PA
CBHW071109250626
47159CB00002B/664